THE BORDER SEARCH

Jack Finch rides out to find the man who killed his young wife. Unknown to him, Dawson Cayne, the man who committed the senseless murder, was working for a revengeful bitter old man, and that included taking out Jack. While recovering from a gunshot wound in a border sanatorium, Connie Kettle makes an appearance, and Jack quickly realizes there is more to his life than trailing a killer. But Cayne wants to prolong the torment, attempting to make Jack pay a dreadful price for a crime he didn't commit . . .

ABE DANCER

THE BORDER SEARCH

Complete and Unabridged

LINFORD
Leicester

First published in Great Britain in 2017 by
Robert Hale
an imprint of The Crowood Press
Wiltshire

First Linford Edition
published 2020
by arrangement with
The Crowood Press
Wiltshire

A catalogue record for this book is available
from the British Library.

ISBN 978–1–4448–4471–9

Published by
Ulverscroft Limited
Anstey, Leicestershire

Set by Words & Graphics Ltd.
Anstey, Leicestershire
Printed and bound in Great Britain by
T. J. International Ltd., Padstow, Cornwall

This book is printed on acid-free paper

1

Jack Finch watched as a scrap of furry mouse scampered to safety beneath the feet of his bayo mare. A moment later, he lifted his gaze and looked south across the barren landscape.

'Let's walk on,' he said, squinting towards the border, the shimmer of distant sun-bleached adobes.

Nearly an hour later a high-noon sun was getting to him, making him tired and scratchy. As he rode into Cerro Cubacho a pair of scrub goats bleated, ran nervously for the shelter of a pole corral. A drowsing *campesino* flicked a toe at a sniffing dog, pushed a finger at the brim of his sombrero. But Jack didn't see much else move and making a sound of encouragement he nudged his mount towards one of the nearest hitch rails.

'*Señor*,' the barkeep acknowledged,

his voice flat and expressionless as Jack entered the low-built, rudimentary cantina.

Jack eyed the jar of pickled eggs, the bowl of chili on the counter in front of him.

'Whiskey. Whatever you've got that passes for it,' he said.

Jack carefully lifted the brimming glass and took a sip, at the same time glancing at the men who were seated at a corner table. They looked like Mexicans, getting drunk. One of them was young and laughing loudly. He wore a range hat, and his boots sported jingly spurs, with which he seemed happy to be making a noise.

A nerve twitched in Jack's cheek. This was the bar where the man who had told him about his wife's murderer had stood. Maybe he had similarly crooked an arm, even spooned an egg from the jar. Jack turned back to the barkeep.

'They drink in here all the time?' he asked.

The barkeep made a half-smile, gave a slight shake of the head.

'No. I don't think so. Then they all look the same to me.'

Jack nodded, considered returning a look of mild amusement.

'I'm looking for someone,' he said. 'A stranger, like me. Perhaps you can recall him? I know he took a drink here recently.'

'He was here until yesterday.'

'Do you know where he is now? Where he went?'

'If it's the gringo, he's on his way back from Sonata.'

'How do you know that?'

'That's where the horses are an' he went to buy one. Besides, he's got a room that's paid up for a few more days. You a friend o' his?'

'Give me the bottle of bug juice while I consider,' Jack said.

Four or five drinks later Jack left the cantina for the beanery he'd noted when tying up. He ate beefsteak and biscuits, drank strong coffee. It seemed likely that he was only hours away from facing the man he'd been hunting down for so many months. There'd be no impulsive killing though, no summary execution. The hurt and anger was too deep for that. As he swallowed the acrid brew shadows lengthened in the street. First dark was approaching, and with tightening nerves he made his way back to the cantina.

Jack deliberately, carefully, snapped a $10 gold coin on to the counter.

'So, I'll be waiting in the gringo's room,' he suggested to the barkeep.

The man sniffed, picked up the coin and deftly secreted it.

'If you didn't know it, his name's Cayne,' he said.

'Well, I want to surprise him,' Jack said in mock conspiracy. 'Might take me a nap, even.' A minute later he was looking around one of two small annexed rooms at the rear of the cantina. He came up with nothing except a single sheet of newsprint slipped under a half-bottle of tequila.

He unfolded the page, moving to a dusty window for more light.

It was a picture from the front of an old *Tucson Messenger*, a group of children waving flags at a summer street party. Jack was among them; he recognized himself standing with two other boys, but that was about all.

'Where the hell did you get this? Are you one of these two?' Jack muttered to the silent walls. 'Did you know me? I don't remember. None of us were more'n knee high. What's going on?'

Try as he might, Jack couldn't put a face to the name: *Cayne*. But he wasn't really interested in knowing more personal stuff about a man he was close to killing.

He replaced the spent cartridge in his Colt, rolled the chamber with his thumb. It was dusk now and the room light was fading fast. His edginess increased and he moved a bamboo chair around the small floor space, setting it between a narrow back door and the window. He sat with his back to the wall, took a few deep breaths and rested his Colt along the top of his right leg.

As the room darkened all sounds seemed to be closing in, becoming more significant; a hoof clopped in the hard-packed dirt of the street; the *borracho's* jingle-bob spurs sounded above the other voices in the bar. Jack wondered if Cayne had already arrived. He twisted around, lifted the edge of a makeshift curtain and looked out of the window. The moon was in its third quarter and if anyone approached close, he would see them quite clearly. Although he'd never seen the man before he was certain he'd know the face when he saw it.

Jack cursed silently, tensed his body at a sound beyond the inner door. He moved the Colt up, waited silently until there was a tentative knock.

'*Señor*. He's here..in the livery,' the barkeep said.

Cautiously, Jack drew the door open. He stood back, levelled his Colt.

'Step in and make a light,' he said.

A match flared and outlined the uneasy Mexican.

'He's brought back a horse. He'll maybe be a while.'

'How do I get to the livery?' Jack asked him.

'You'll see it. It's across the street . . . almost. Whatever you're set to do, do it there. My business here is bad enough.'

The match died and in the darkness Jack tapped the man's bony shoulder with the long barrel of the Colt. 'If you're thinking of giving this man Cayne any sort of warning, remember it's my money you've already tucked away. Next time it might be a bullet. *Comprendes?* Now, open this door,' he added, turning the barkeep around.

'*Sí señor.*'

Jack stepped into the moonlight. He waited until the door closed behind him, then moved quickly to the corner of the building and through to the front street, until he was in a doorway almost opposite the livery.

A lamp deep inside the building lit a grass-strewn dirt floor, two horses in stalls and a shambling, bulky figure who was talking to someone off in the shadows.

Jack holstered his Colt, wiped the palm of his hand and pulled the gun again. As he was about to cross the street a man reeled into the doorway in front of him. Jack cursed, took a short step sideways.

'What do you want?' the drunk rasped. 'Waitin' up on a man.'

'I don't want anything. Just keep quiet,' Jack snapped, shoving him aside. The man grabbed at Jack's gun hand for support and Jack had to hit him hard in the back of his neck. The man collapsed and Jack kneed him to the ground, back into the doorway.

When Jack looked up he saw that across the street the livery man had heard the scuffle and was looking directly his way.

Pushing his Colt back down into his

holster Jack hastily crossed the street. He wanted to get in quick before the man thought about what was happening; he didn't want him to say anything.

'Evenin',' he said, coming up with something the man could respond to. 'I saw you inside, talking to someone.'

'Me talkin'? Oh sure, yeah. He's back in the stalls, rubbin' his horse down.'

'Keep your eye on the street. There's drunks abroad and they're looking for trouble,' Jack said tersely. He went straight on into the livery, but very alert, loosening his Colt. There were no sounds except one of the horses snorting, the other farting in response. Under the lantern's yellow light he drew back the Colt's hammer, halting beside an empty stall when a stick cracked under his boot. The horses took it in turns to nicker at his approach.

Jack glanced into each of the empty stalls, moving slowly into the gloom beyond the lamp's beams. Thoughtful, he stopped and held his breath, listening intently.

He heard nothing; at the same time he felt a draught of cool air brush his face. He walked forward, peering beyond the open back door. The stockyards, under a mantle of pale silvery light, appeared empty.

'It was him,' he muttered under his breath. 'And if he's hiding in there, he's close to being dead,' he added, noting a long stock shed at the rear of the empty yards.

His skin felt cold, shivery, as he scanned the cattle chutes, climbing through a pole fence into a second yard, through to a third on his way to the shed.

His eyes grew accustomed to the darkness between the close rails of the pens and he could see a hanging assortment of ropes and straps. It was where they slaughtered cattle they couldn't sell: the buzzard baits and runt calves. A sweet, musty smell of animal odours infused every square inch of the ground, and Jack couldn't help thinking it wasn't a place you would want to be at high noon.

He felt a churn of his vitals, hoped the chili would stay down. Then he cursed vehemently as he recalled Annie, her small face drained of life, hideously disfigured by one big bullet hole. Her slaughter was little different from that meted out to worthless cattle.

'Getting past me's going to be the most difficult thing you ever done, feller,' Jack said into the silence. 'And staying alive's not an option.' He angrily confronted the darkness, listened for a moment, looked charily at mesquite piled high against the corral rails.

'You've somehow doubled back, you son of a bitch. I must've passed you,' he added, seeing that the iron sliding-bolt was still securing the shed door. Having searched the whole yard he turned and ran to the front of the building again, where he confronted the liveryman, who was, obviously nervously, waiting for his return.

'He came back,' Jack stated breath-lessly.

'You talkin' about the man Cayne, señor?'

'You know I am, goddamnit! Where the hell did he go?'

'Towards the cantina.'

'Front or back?'

'Front, I think.'

★   ★   ★

Jack was thinking; if Cayne had entered the cantina, there was no reason to go in any other way than from the front. The man knew full well where his adversary was, where he was coming from. *You'd go straight to your room, collect your pouch and anything else lying around, then hightail it, I guess. In the darkness, most likely set up a bushwhack, and not too far away,* were Jack's next thoughts.

Facing the outside of Cayne's door, Jack prepared himself to snatch and drag it open. Then, for the shortest time, his mind realized the things he should have considered a moment or two earlier.

He knows I've followed him from the livery to the cantina. He's probably watched from the shadows and trailed me around to the rear of the building, Jack thought. *He'll have the drop on me as I confront the back door to his room. Yeah, the bushwhack — and earlier than I'd expected.* Jack was making a low curse at the inevitability of what was going to happen next when the steel muzzle pressed hard into the base of his neck.

'Drop your gun,' Cayne said.

With almost uncontrollable frustration Jack was ready to ignore the command. But the sharp snap of an action being set brought back reason, and he let his own Colt slip to the ground.

'That's good,' the man breathed. 'Stayin' alive has become an option after all.'

Out of the corner of an eye, Jack dimly saw the man's head, his broad shoulders.

'Move any more an' you'll get your face whipped,' Cayne said. 'What's your interest in me?'

'You killed my wife,' Jack muttered. 'That good enough?'

There was a quick intake of breath, then a long moment's silence. 'Then you'll be the one I *meant* to kill,' Cayne said. 'You remember Will Morgan an' Bean Decker? They were friends o' yours.'

Jack now realized who those figures were who had been standing either side of him in the picture.

'And *my wife* was some sort of collateral damage? Is that it?' he rasped. 'So what happened to Will and Bean?' Jack guessed it would be the same fate as his Annie's. But he still had no idea what it all meant, how it all tied in.

'Swimmin' downstream in the Gila. There certainly ain't goin' to be no reunion,' Cayne said. 'But in the here

14

an' now, the man I've been lookin' for's come lookin' for me. Is this serendipity or what?'

'I don't know what the hell you're talking about, mister. What is this?' Jack asked.

'Don't raise your voice,' Cayne replied abruptly, jabbing the barrel of the Colt. 'That pair o' young turkeys said more or less the same as you. That innocence . . . pretendin' an' all. You remember San Simon?'

Thinking it might set him up for a move, Jack let his shoulders relax a little.

'San Simon? Up on the border?' he replied.

'Yeah. Where my cousin cashed in.'

'That's tough. But I don't know you or your brother from Adam,' Jack protested.

The gun barrel lifted to touch his ear and a chilly shiver passed between his shoulder blades and down the middle of his back.

'This'll make it all three o' you. Or

four, the way you'd have seen it,' Cayne said. 'You can go sleep with the other catfish tonight,' he added needlessly.

The message to react had reached Jack's muscles. He was primed for a fast turn, his fingertips set for a swift upward movement. In a simultaneous, affecting blur, he'd seen the image of a white calico dress fluttering among waves of yellow corn, the pale hands of his wife, clutching out at nothing.

'Why don't you . . . ?' he started. It was a desperate attempt to slow Cayne for a fraction of a second, give the man's mind something to consider before pulling the trigger.

Jack had already started his calculated move when someone else's voice filled the moment.

'Hey, you two? *Que esto?*'

Jack felt the intense pressure of Cayne's gun barrel withdraw. There was more shouting and he whirled around, moved away from the door as it swung open. The cantina's barkeep stepped through. He was holding a lantern up

16

against the darkness.

'He was here?' he asked of Jack. 'Señor Cayne was here?'

'Yes, goddamn it. He got around me at the livery . . . was just about to blow my head apart.' Jack swung round and stared at the group of men who had closed in from the street, now moving closer. 'Where the hell is he?' he grated. 'One of you saw him . . . where he went.'

The barkeep shook his head. 'No one sees or says much around here, señor. Trouble don't usually come with one hand.'

Jack looked closer at the men, whose expressions and intentions were unreadable in the darkness. He picked up his Colt, seeing that Cayne wasn't able to get a clear shot at him, and stepped around the Mexican to glance into the empty, rented store room. He saw the newspaper picture of himself with Will Morgan and Bean Decker.

Five minutes later Jack was out front of the cantina, quartering the street and the low buildings.

'He'll be out there considering his options, taking advantage of the night,' he muttered. 'I'll wager that new mount wasn't too bedded down, either.' He pushed the .44 Colt into his holster, knew even a sharpshooter wouldn't be able to hit Cayne if and when he went by on his ride out of town. If I wasn't before, I really am into bushwhack territory now, he was thinking.

2

A flat stretch of land dotted with desert willow and paint-brush gradually gave way to more rocky, boulder-strewn country.

Jack dismounted. Not wanting to be diverted by any ground shadows or night movements, he closed his eyes to concentrate. He heard the sound he was likely chasing, but it was too far away, getting even fainter as it made higher ground, the foothills of the Magdalenas. He sensed that his quarry had now become the hunter, drawing him onwards for the ambush.

Jack's stemwinder watch said it was a quarter-hour past midnight. Wispy clouds started to thicken across the sky and, when moonlight faded altogether, he made coldharbour camp beside a big, silvery smoketree. He tethered his mare, put down his saddle and bedroll.

'Cayne won't be going anywhere either,' he muttered. Unable to sleep, he got to thinking, wondering what it was that he, Bean and Will could have done to make Cayne kill. Jack had only been about ten years old, so it wasn't for playing truant or feeding strips of hog fat to the sheriff's geese.

*   *   *

The sky lightened, but the temperature dropped nearly thirty degrees before the sun broke across the peaks of the distant mountain ranges.

Jack pulled a pair of leather gloves over his chilled hands, risked a small fire from a few handfuls of tumbleweed. Ten minutes later, cursing at the protest growls from his empty belly, he repacked his light traps and saddled up.

Ahead of him, a high, sharp ridge of sandstone drew his attention. *There'd be a fair view of the badlands from up there*, he thought. 'For a goddamn goat,' he added quietly, and turned his mount towards a ridge that sloped more gradually up from the arid ground.

A mile on, and he ground-hitched the bay and drew his rifle, scrambled on to the slope that led up to the lookout. He knelt a hundred feet above his mare, his breath hanging in fine clouds, his eyes sweeping the barren country for any sign of movement. He watched a big turkey vulture soaring above a distant ridge. The bird was on patrol, waiting for the day's first rise of warming air.

'You're not dead yet, then, wherever you are,' he breathed quietly of Cayne's situation.

His attention shifted to a sudden disturbance on a narrow outcrop ten feet or so below him. He saw a definite movement, looked like curling ribbons of shadow. He flattened himself and wriggled close to the edge of the ridge, bit off the glove of his right hand and stuffed it in his shirt pocket. He lowered the elevation of the rifle, squinted along its barrel down at the nest of rattlesnakes.

No one's disturbed you. You're getting ready for the sun, he thought and shivered with revulsion. He tensed his finger against the rifle's trigger and twisted around for a nervy look behind him.

The sun rose higher, the night's chill started to get burned off. Jack squinted, searching for any sign of movement out on the sandy wasteland.

Either you're well gone or you're holed up behind one of those smoketree brakes, he thought. *Aren't you?* He drew in his knees, pushed himself up into a crouch. There was no doubting the bang of a big bore rifle, the loud smack as the bullet hit the stock of his Winchester.

Jack cursed as his rifle left his grip, bouncing once before tumbling to the rattlers below him. He gasped as a second bullet whined and fizzed close overhead. He took a deep breath, quickly pulled his Colt as he twisted and turned to face the other way. He made himself as flat as he could, tried to estimate where the shots came from. It was somewhere behind him and to his left, the direction he'd ridden from, and he knew the shooter.

'Twice, so it's my fault,' he muttered anxiously as reverberations of the gunshots continued to whirl around him. 'You've gone and got behind me again.'

He rolled on to his left shoulder, wincing at the pain. He rolled back, saw the dark stain in the dirt. A shard of rock had sliced upward into the fleshy part of his forearm and it hurt. It didn't disable him, but bright blood was running freely on to his wrist, across the back of his hand. He drew in his shoulders and hunched up a few inches, cursed as bullets spat and ricocheted around his body. There was a brief pause, then more firing kept him pinned down.

'Hell! I wasn't born to this goddamn work. I wanted a quick kill,' he rasped, the words gumming in his parched mouth.

Jack thought for a moment, guessed that Cayne, had somehow managed to climb above him. That meant he was perched high on the sandstone ridge that Jack had earlier decided was too steep to climb.

If I sit up real quick, watch closely, perhaps I'll get a glimpse of him as he breaks his cover, he thought. If he gets to see me to shoot, I'll get to see him. And a fat load of good that'll do me.

As fast as he could, and in one continuous movement, Jack rolled on to his back and bent up from the waist. He looked to the south, close to where he estimated Cayne was in cover. He saw what he wanted, the dark, shifting shape of the man. Then he saw the flash, felt the bullet as it burned and snatched its way across the side of his neck.

Yeah, it's you all right. All I've got to do now is slip down into the nest of rattlers, ask for my gun back, then give as good as I'm getting, he was thinking before everything closed down to black.

★   ★   ★

The pungent smells of wood smoke and roasting meat drew Jack from the darkness.

'D'you think he'll get up?' a voice asked.

'Yeah, sometime. They're not much more'n flesh bites,' came the reply.

Jack stirred, blinked some focus and feeling back, cursed at the pains in his head, shoulders, arms and legs.

'Flesh bites to you, mister, whoever the hell you are,' he said, not too forcefully.

Beyond and way above the fire stars peppered the deep sky. On the ground low flames were licking at a piece of spiked meat. Three men were close in to the firelight, heavy shadows playing across their features. One of them was the young drunk Jack had last seen in the cantina, the one who wore jingle-bob spurs. Jack allowed himself to slip back into the tranquillity of nothingness again, the dark, warm place where he seemed to be safe and secure.

When his senses stirred again pains and a rasping thirst brought him back to near full consciousness.

'Our lucky friend's comin' back to us,' one of the men said.

Wincing at the chew of pain, Jack raised his head.

'Water . . . please,' he croaked out. 'Something to drink.'

Someone held Jack's head while he sucked at the lip of a tin mug. The coffee tasted almost as bad as the cantina's whiskey. He struggled against the pain of swallowing as it burned its way down his throat.

'Easy, *amigo*. Ha! He's just like a new calf on the teat,' the man said.

The young Texan stepped closer, kneeling to speak.

'We patched you up best we could. We all thought you were dead meat when we found you up there.'

The recollection of getting shot quickly filtered into Jack's mind.

'Did you see him — any sign?' he asked.

'You talkin' of the man who did this? The *fusilero*?' The Texan shook his head. 'No, *amigo*. He must've heard us comin', been well gone. We heard the shots though. Found your horse an' figured out where you were. Who is he, this person who's not an obvious friend?'

He probably heard your goddamn jingle-bobs, Jack thought.

'He calls himself Cayne . . . don't know if that's his real name or not . . . or what the hell he wants,' Jack muttered, the emotions of frustration and fear making his vitals shiver. 'But he's out there still. I know that.' He gazed concernedly into the darkness and gritted his teeth. 'Have you any water?'

The Mexican pushed the saddle further up against Jack's back.

27

'Drink some more coffee, *amigo*, then tell me . . . tell us, about this man.'

'I just told you all I know. He's name's Cayne. And right now he's bearing some sort of grudge against me.'

'*Sí*, a real powerful one. So, we can take you to a town near the border. There's a doctor, even a one-horse hospital the Arizona Raiders used to use.'

'Thanks.' Jack relaxed his head into the saddle. 'I saw you in the cantina at Cerro Cubacho,' he said, fixing his eyes on the young Mexican. 'About three, four days ago, a tall, big-shouldered Anglo was there too. Corn hair. Do you recall?'

'It sounds like I would if I'd been there. But no, *amigo*. I don't.'

Jack gave a weak, single nod. 'Yeah. Apparently everyone says more or less that.'

The youngster produced a flat bottle of tequila and drew the cork.

'We got no white man's physic, but

this might help.'

Jack took the bottle and tipped a measure into his mouth. The drink was strong and warming, brought some life forces back. He looked to the roasting meat.

'I wouldn't say no to a cut of whatever you got cooking,' he said.

Grinning, the other Mexican used a thin-bladed skinner to slice off a portion of dark meat.

'You must be on the mend to want this,' the man said, extending a morsel to Jack. 'Got a name we can use?'

'Jack Finch,' Jack replied. 'I was obviously never that broke, just had the goddamn stuffing knocked from me. I feel like hell though. What is this stuff?' he asked.

'Dog, snake, skunk. Roasted for long enough, it don't really matter.'

The meat and cactus juice proved a little rich and fifteen minutes later Jack had gut spasms as well as the shakes. He started shivering again, even though they draped another blanket over him.

'When did you reckon on making that infirmary?' he groaned.

'Early tomorrow. With lots o' things on our side, no later than noon.'

Jack was in pain. He was losing the feeling of his left arm and fingers. Thinking he could find the dark, warm comforts of oblivion again, he closed his eyes, but nothing came. The other men appeared to be snuggled down, sniffing and snoring. Jack remained awake, seeing the fire collapse to white-and-grey ash.

It seemed he had been given a second chance to get away, although his wounds might yet fester and kill him. He listened to a coyote barking mournfully. It was from many miles away up on a rock, and he thought he knew how the lone animal felt.

'Yeah, you an' me both,' he muttered. 'What's it all about?'

As he lay very still the pain in Jack's body eased a little, but not enough to let him sleep. His distressed mind took him back to the wheatfield, the bright sun, the barn door swinging eerily in the wind, the flutter of Annie's calico dress. He hadn't wanted to look at her, but he had to know. A single bullet had blown away half of her small face. To anybody other than Jack she was unrecognizable. It was the start of what had set him on the ride to Cerro Cubacho.

'I've heard of the man you're looking for,' the man had told him. 'He was tall . . . taller than most. A mess o' yellow hair.'

It was the connection that brought Jack from his reverie. The barkeep hadn't got it wrong, as Jack thought he might have done.

'Hell! The man's name *is* Cayne,' he hissed on full waking. 'And his first name is Dawson.'

Jack now recalled a straggly, fair-haired kid who had dogged an older brother, whose name was Lew. To Jack, Lew had been a sort of childhood hero, a figure of near-rapscallion repute. For some reason Jack was thinking of

Tucson, but that had been twenty-five years ago. Whatever it was with Cayne must have happened before then. It was something from when they lived in San Simon, because that's where Jack knew Dawson and Lew from.

Jack recalled young, hazy faces, one or two incidents of junior skylarking. Images of his dead parents broke in again, then Annie, and the reality of Dawson Cayne returned.

'What the hell's going on?' he muttered in a low voice for the umpteenth time. He looked around to see if anyone had heard him.

When the coyote finally stopped howling Jack grew tense at the massive silence. It was close to dawn. There was no colour yet, but the top line of the distant sierras grew visible in the east.

One of the Mexicans yawned loudly. He kicked off his blanket and stood up, looking curiously toward a fluttering disturbance in the brush.

'Goddamn bobwhites!' Jack breathed.

'We're all here, so what the hell's set 'em off?'

The Mexican froze. They saw nothing but in the half-light they heard the dull thrum of departing hoofbeats.

'Devil's nightmare,' Jack mouthed, sitting up stiffly. 'He's been right here and he knows I'm still kicking.'

3

The big rising sun made Jack feel bad as they rode for the Arizona border. They had tied him on to his mare so that he couldn't fall.

'We got your rifle back,' said the young Mexican who had introduced himself as Carlos Rebo. 'It's lost some of its good looks, but it'll still shoot.' Rebo was riding alongside because of Jack's unsteadiness. 'Something else wrong, *amigo*?' he queried.

'I'm thinking he's riding one of those ridges,' Jack said. 'For another hour he's got the sun high and behind him. Where else is he going to be?'

Rebo squinted at a distant parallel ridge.

'I guess it's where any of us would be if we were trailin' you,' he replied with a grim smile. 'But don't worry, *amigo*. He's got to be some crazy *hombre* to tackle four of us. You should be safe enough.'

'He's already shot close enough for me to worry. I reckon that's a big ol' Henry he's carrying, so, maybe we should make some distance . . . raise more dust.'

'It's up to you, *amigo*. You think you can ride like that?'

'I'd prefer to die trying,' Jack replied with a wit he didn't feel. '*Vamonos*.'

Rebo considered for a moment before heading his sorrel in a more northerly direction across the huge sand basin. It was a move intended to give Dawson Cayne less of a vantage point if he wanted another shot at Jack.

Line abreast, the four riders stayed in open ground. Rebo knew that the shimmering heat off the desert floor would make moving figures an almost impossible target for a distant hunter.

Jack clenched his teeth against the hurt when he twisted in the saddle. He constantly thought he saw figures rising from the haze, wobbling for a moment before disappearing again. He cursed when he noticed he was falling behind the others and heeled the bayo mare for more speed. His neck wound was bleeding again and his left arm was sending pain up to join it. His strength was fading fast by the time he saw his Mexican rescuers grouping around him.

Strong fingers untied the rope that stopped Jack falling to the ground. They eased him from the saddle, carried him to the shadier side of an old sotol. Most of his shirt was soaked dark from fevery sweat and the blood from his neck and arm.

'That looks bad,' the older Mexican said. 'Maybe I can stop the bleeding.'

'Make it quick. If there is a shooter out there we've all become sittin' targets,' Rebo said, the concern clear in his voice. 'Here,' he went on, putting the tequila bottle close to Jack's mouth. 'You can die tryin' to get roostered.'

★　★　★

When Jack regained consciousness he was lying under a neatly tucked clean sheet. A bottle of water and a drinking-glass were standing on a side table. His neck and right arm were bandaged, the smell in his nostrils was pungent and carbolicky. The pain in his body had subsided to a dull throb, and he moved his right arm to try and push himself into a sitting position.

'No need. You're not going anywhere,' a feminine voice said firmly.

Jack was surprised to see a young woman in a nurse's uniform rise from a chair cater-corner to the foot of the bed. She moved towards him, shaking her head.

'We had trouble stopping you bleeding, Mr Jack. Give some respect to those who have saved you.'

He lay back on the pillow, offered a feeble, contrite smile.

'Sorry. It doesn't happen that often.'

The nurse had an olive-skinned, brown-eyed face, but it was her hair that held Jack's attention. It was glossy black, plaited like the tarred rope of a Rio Grande steamboat. Jack thought of Annie, felt an immediate grip of guilt.

He cleared his throat.

'The men who brought me here?' he said. 'Do you know where they are?'

'They didn't say. Only that they will wait to find out how you are. You are lucky they brought you here.'

'Yeah.' Jack looked at the drawn-curtained windows, not for the first time, wondered what indication they suggested as to his predicament.

'Is it night?' he asked.

'Yes.'

'Where are we?'

'Whitewater. The Whitewater Sanatorium.'

'Not New Mexico?'

'Not quite. Arizona.'

Jack blinked, held his eyes shut for a long moment.

'How long have I been here?' he asked.

'Four hours. You were brought in at three o'clock.'

Jack looked around to see where his clothes were.

'They are in the laundry room,' she said, as if reading his thoughts.

Looking to see if I've got the dollars to pay, he thought.

'I hope you're not running a bar of soap over my Colt,' he offered instead. She gave a tolerant smile.

'That's safe. There is no need for a gun in here.'

'I'd like to be the judge of that,' Jack said. 'The man who did this won't be too concerned with your hospital etiquette. How many armed guards you got outside?' he added facetiously.

'No patient is allowed firearms. It's our way. I'll ask someone to come and see you.'

'Someone? What does that mean?'

'Someone senior . . . the director. But if you *are* in some sort of danger it's the concern of everyone here. When Doctor Cooper has taken care of your neck and your arm we will get you sorted out.'

Jack gave a resigned, exhausted sigh.

'I haven't even got my boots on,' he said and lay back down.

★ ★ ★

A large strip of white canvas had been stretched between two wooden beams above where Jack lay. He guessed it was to reflect the light from a cluster of twelve happy-jack lanterns, hanging close. He knew exactly how many because, from his bed, he'd been counting them. Likewise he knew the number of silvery steel instruments arranged neatly in the tray of a nearby trolley. He was sort of thankful he didn't know what they were for.

The hospital's Dr Cooper came in eventually, accompanied by the nurse with the black shiny hair. Doctor Cooper was a thin, businesslike middle-aged man.

He acknowledged Jack with a brisk nod.

'Some things are best tended to, Mr Jack. Our health is one of them. The neck wound is close to your carotid artery and the tear in your arm is very dirty. Each of those must be both cleaned and dressed properly, to avoid septic poisoning.'

'I understand,' Jack said stiffly. 'But right now it's a different sort of sepsis I'm worried about.' A little earlier Jack had been given laudanum and now he felt more dopey than sleepy.

'Have you taken this before, Mr Jack?' the nurse asked, dripping the sedative on to a fold of cloth and holding it to his nose. 'Breathe normally. It helps with the discomfort — the nervousness,' she said with a thoughtful smile.

'Like I've been telling you, it's not getting cleaned up I'm nervous about. I hope my new friends are watching the door,' Jack replied quietly. 'You haven't come across someone called Cayne have you?' he asked as the overhead lamps merged and went out.

It was later the same night when he awoke. He could hear the thumping of his heart but felt no immediate pain. He was trying to break away from the nightmare, the vision of somebody reaching in to where the curtains had been drawn back, the window opening. In his terror he had rolled away, fallen from the bed and crashed to the floor. There he remained, very still, fearful because he didn't know what had happened, uncertain of any of his senses.

4

'Mr Jack, are you awake? Can you hear me?'

Jack nodded. The words seemed to come from far away, somehow disconnected, not meant for him. Early sunshine struck the ceiling and two of the far walls. The window curtains were pulled back, which took Jack's almost immediate attention. Outside, the thick branches of a jacaranda climbed alongside a veranda post.

That would be what I saw last night then, Jack thought wryly. The Dawson Cayne tree.

'Did you fall from your bed last night?' the nurse continued.

Jack's impulse was to tell the whole truth.

'I didn't sleep too well,' he replied, thinking that that was at least half of it.

'Lucky you're strong,' she said. 'And

lucky there's nothing broken.'

'Maybe you should hog-tie me,' he said.

The nurse smiled. Her raven hair was again dressed in a thick plait, hanging to one side of her brown-eyed face.

'I wouldn't know how,' she said. 'Tying splints and bandages is what I'm good at.'

'Yeah. How long before someone returns me my clothes?'

'You will have to take that up with Dr Cooper. But I would have thought soon,' she replied. 'There's nothing life-threatening. Are you staying in Mexico?'

'I wasn't far from staying for good a short while ago. There's something I've got to do . . . getting more important. So it'll be for a while, I guess.'

A frown crossed the nurse's forehead.

'So you can take someone's life?'

'I meant it was important that I defend myself,' Jack said gruffly.

'I think that's an opportune difference, Mr Jack.'

Jack shut his eyes for a moment. 'Then it's best we leave it at that. And my last name's Finch.'

'Very well.' The nurse returned his curtness. 'After you've eaten some food I think you'll be having visitors. The men who brought you here,' she added in the way of someone who cared but didn't want to show it.

'Thank you for that, ma'am,' Jack replied in a similar manner.

Opening the door, the nurse turned and gave him a long look.

'I'm a nurse, not a ma'am. And you might like to know it was the hospital *porter* who found you weren't in bed, last night.'

Jack glared. 'He didn't come in through the window, did he?'

'No, of course he didn't. What do you mean?'

'Nothing. At least I know there was somebody there. I wasn't scuttling under the bed for nothing.'

'Whatever the meaning of that may be, Mr Jack, I think we should ease up on the laudanum.' With a faint smile across her face, the nurse closed the door.

Jack was relieved that his night visitor hadn't been Dawson Cayne. It was almost funny that he'd been in hiding, cringing with fear of the janitor, and the nurse seemed to know it. Minutes later an older woman, a civil helper, brought him a platter of grits and eggs. She sat quietly, watching him eat, encouraging him the moment he took a breather.

'That was all good. Thank you,' he told her when she was pouring him a glass of warm goat milk. 'What's the name of the nurse?'

'You mean Connie?' she said without looking up. 'Constanza Kettle.'

'I've been too ill to take much notice of her.'

'I've never known a man too ill not to notice his nurse, Mr Jack.'

'Yeah, well,' Jack started. 'I think she said there's *hombres* waiting outside. Will you please tell them they can come in.'

Jack was still chewing over his predicament when young Carlos Rebo and his two sidekicks entered the room.

'Hey *amigo*,' the young Mexican greeted Jack.

Jack shook his hand and exchanged nods with the other two.

'I reckon I owe you for bringing me here . . . waiting to see how it turns out,' he said. He remembered his pa once saying: *when in a tricky situation don't ask a question that's likely to put you in a worse one.* Jack didn't think that right now was the time to ask Rebo: *why?*

Having had his wounds tended to, eaten the decent breakfast, Jack was feeling much better. If Dawson Cayne hadn't pursued him to Whitewater, that only helped.

'Incidentally, did you see any sign of my deadly friend after I blacked out? Any sign at all?' he asked.

'If there was, *señor*, we didn't see it, an' we're good at seeing,' one of the other two said. 'But we were in a hurry to get here — good reason, eh?'

'Perhaps he's scuttled back into the hole he crawled out of,' Jack muttered.

'Maybe, maybe not,' Rebo said. 'I'm curious, *amigo*. This Cayne *hombre*? You say he had some sort o' grudge against you . . . a score to settle?'

Jack gave a little shake of his head.

'I think it's something he made up. I've recalled who he is though. He had an older brother named Lew. I guess to kids last names aren't that important.'

'You must have done something wrong . . . done him some harm. His brother, maybe?'

'No, I'd have remembered that. Anyhow, Lew's dead.'

'What happened?' Rebo asked.

Taking his mind back, Jack drew out an image.

'He got thrown from a big, snorty claybank. He landed badly, bust lotsa stuff inside him. There was nothing anybody could do. It was an accident.'

'Then there's got to be something else. Think again,' Rebo suggested.

'No. We sort of admired Lew Cayne. Taken with him, I suppose . . . even influenced. He always had that bit more gen about stuff . . . everything.'

'Who were the others? You said *we*.'

'That was Bean and Will. It was usually the three of us.'

'Will Morgan?'

Jack tensed, didn't answer. Of a sudden his mind was racing in many directions. The young Mexican was too intense in his questioning, and he'd provided a name he shouldn't have known.

'Assuming you're not spirits of the Gila Desert, you must know I'm going to ask this, sometime . . . ' he started. Then, 'Who the hell are you?' he asked more sharply.

Rebo sighed, gave a tolerant smile.

'I'm sure if you hadn't got so much on your mind you would have asked before now, *amigo*,' he replied. 'I'm a US marshal an' these two are deputies, Rafael and Magro. We have been hired to investigate a murder that happened in San Simon last year. I'm sorry to tell you, your old friend Will Morgan is dead.'

Jack held his thoughts steady. Rebo's disclosure had answered one or two questions, like, how they knew about the hospital and what Rafael meant by being good at seeing.

'You don't look like any goddamn marshal or law officers I ever saw,' he said, nevertheless.

'I wouldn't get far in my line of work if I did, *amigo*,' Rebo answered. 'There would be too many closing doors.'

'I did hear about Will being dead,' Jack went on. 'What's that to do with you being in border country?'

'I've been trailing Dawson Cayne,' the young marshal continued. 'That's why I was in Cerro Cubacho. I thought I had him cornered — would have, too, if someone else hadn't horned in. So, now that we've put most of our cards on the table, why do *you* want him?'

'He killed my wife,' Jack replied flatly.

'I wasn't there at the time, so he shot *her* instead.'

Rebo pulled off his range hat. 'I'm sorry, *amigo*. I had no idea,' he said.

'I know you didn't,' Jack responded.

'The other boy..Bean?'

'Yeah, Bean Decker. Cayne said he'd killed him too.'

'You rule yourself out, it was one of them did something wrong,' Rebo suggested. 'Meantime, we'll all stick a bit closer.'

'I don't want any nursemaids, and I'm not your goddamn bait, either,' Jack grated. 'I set out to get the man who killed my wife. Nothing's changed.

'It can't be your summary justice, *amigo*. Even if it *is* deserved. He'll be tried at Tucson for his crimes and then hanged.'

The two men locked resolute eyes.

'If you are going to get in my way, mister, remember I'm the one who carries the memory of Annie with half her face shot away.'

The lawman stood uneasily twisting his range hat.

'It's not the sort of thing to argue over, and I do understand,' he said. 'But if you set out to catch him the way you are now, *he* will likely shoot you. *Buen dia*.' Rebo motioned for the deputies to follow him. As he left the room the jingling of his spurs didn't seem to Jack to be quite so noticeable.

'Now it's no guns and no body-guards. Well done, Jack!' he muttered.

5

During the next few days Jack saw the lawmen from time to time as he sat on the hospital's raised front veranda. The two-way acknowledgement was usually the raising of a hat, the lift of a hand. Beyond the low, flat rooftops, he could see a vast tract of sand, mesquite and brush that stretched for fifty miles.

Not much to gain by chasing a shadow across desert wasteland. I've done that, he thought. He was beginning to think that maybe Cayne had given up on him, that seeing him in company with three armed Mexicans had perhaps scared him off. But that was illusory; not a minute passed when he didn't curse or react to an unfamiliar sound.

Constanza Kettle was very attentive. Apart from an ageing city dweller suffering from tuberculosis and a youngster with a broken leg, Jack was the only incumbent of Whitewater Sanatorium.

Consequently she often sat and talked with him towards the end of a day.

'You could stay here,' she put to him one evening. 'If, like you say, your needs aren't great, there's work enough. You could start over, make a new life.'

'I know you mean well, Connie, but right now I don't think the sort of work this neck of the woods offers is a viable option,' Jack replied. 'Besides, I'm not looking for a new life just yet.'

'Yes. I did mean well, Jack,' she said. 'I would hardly be thinking of anything else.' Looking a little more hurt than bothered, Connie picked up an empty coffee cup and left.

Jack gave the idea of a relationship with Connie a moment's thought, then returned his attention to his fighting corner. He recalled that Bean Decker's dad and his own had been friends; like many others they had at one time

54

actually worked for the Cayne family. He had an idea his pa had been fired by a senior family member, but didn't know who or why. If it were true, maybe it would have been Cayne's father. Putting the fragmented memories away, Jack stood up and stretched. He flexed the fingers of his right hand, then the muscles of his neck. He knew he was being watched from the nearby cantina by Carlos Rebo and his men.

'What a way to earn a crust,' he muttered. 'Becoming a pest, too.' He smiled coldly, raised his right hand, extended two straight fingers and feigned three gunshots in their direction. He picked up his Winchester with the broken stock and walked back into the hospital.

'Nurse — Connie. Have you got a few moments?' he called out on the way to his room.

'What's the matter?' Connie asked a minute later.

'Nothing an' everything,' Jack

replied. 'I've done some quick think-ing, though. Maybe you're right about me doing something else. What do you suggest?'

'I'd already done my thinking, Jack. My father has cattle and some horses and you know about stock. This time of year he's always short-handed. You wouldn't be a charity case or anything.'

'As long as I'm not expected to go breaking in any young broncos. But if I go, I'll leave when Rebo and his friends are looking the other way. You'll probably have to think up some sort of story.'

'I understand, Jack. Señor Rebo told me about your wife.'

'He was wrong to do that.'

'Perhaps. But I'm sorry anyway.'

'OK. I'll leave tonight. Later at full dark. Thanks, Connie, and tell no one of this. No one. That *could* be real harmful to my health.'

★ ★ ★

Jack was tense, but he'd been waiting coolly in the dark. To anyone still watching, he had been tucked up and fast asleep for a couple of hours. When Connie came for him, just before midnight, he opened the door and stepped out, silently followed her to the rear of the building.

Connie unlocked a sturdy oak door, moved into the dark, starry night.

'There's a horse standing saddled beyond the old oak,' she said. 'Ride straight south for six miles. Pick up the Nogales coach at the stage station and buy a ticket to Aqua Cajon. Someone there can take you out to Pa's ranch. It's not far. Here.' She pressed an old acorn into his palm. 'It must have been blessed to last such a long time. Keep it with you. *Bona fortuna.*'

Turning it over in his hand, Jack ran his thumb around the dried-out casing before dropping it in his pocket.

'Thank you, but I'll try and not to trust to it. Sorry,' he added, avoiding her eyes. 'I've got too much on my mind right now to come up with better.'

'Then come back when you have.'

'Yeah, I will,' he grunted at Connie's agreeable suggestion. 'Could you see my mare's looked after?'

A minute later Jack stretched out a hand to a chestnut gelding. Carefully, he swung up and astride the saddle, flicked the reins and gave a gentle heel.

He rode out behind the buildings for a while, took a passing, disinterested glance at Whitewater's back yards. At the outskirts of the town, by what looked like grain stores and a pole corral, he swung west for the cover of a cedar brake. He drew rein and took a long glance back at both ends of the main street, gave Carlos Rebo a second thought.

To Jack's way of thinking, the young Mexican lawman was making some curious decisions about trailing a killer. He made a doubtful smile, heeled his mount from the trees towards the southerly trail.

The moon would be good for five

hours' riding, but he'd only need thirty minutes to make the swing station and the Nogales mail coach. Screened in his ride from the sanatorium and Rebo's attention, Jack felt sure no one except Connie would be wise to his departure.

*   *   *

Carlos Rebo looked at the moon hanging almost directly above the cedar brake, and cursed. He sensed he was missing something but he wasn't certain what.

Twice that night he had seen Nurse Kettle in the window directly across from him. Taking everything into account, which wasn't much in the darkness, he supposed she could only be looking to see if he was still there. He'd thought her behaviour odd because she hadn't done so on previous nights.

'You're over *there*, checking to see that I'm over *here*, but why? Why tonight?' he muttered. 'What's our mutual friend Jack Finch up to?'

Seconds later Rebo was tugging the bell chain at the front door of the sanatorium.

At that late hour the main street was deserted and, other than for the noises from night critters, practically silent. Rebo gave the bell another, more impatient pull.

It was Connie who opened the door. Rebo instinctively touched the brim of his sombrero, gave one of his most attractive smiles.

'Sorry to disturb you at this time, Nurse Kettle, but I saw you were still up,' the Mexican said. 'There's something I'd like to see Jack Finch about. It's a law thing . . . quite urgent.'

'At midnight it must be. I don't think . . . ' she began, but Rebo was already pushing past her.

'Oh, it really is,' Rebo muttered, hurrying straight to the room where Jack was supposedly still a walking wounded. On opening the door he could see, even in the gloomy light from

60

the hallway, that the bed and room were empty.

'When did he leave?' he demanded impatiently.

Connie wanted to look away, say nothing, but she lowered her eyes to her hand lamp.

'Ma'am, you know I'm a US lawman, who's trying to protect Jack from a killer.'

'There is no killer here,' she said firmly. 'I think the both of you are running to and from ghosts.'

'Sorry, ma'am, those wounds of his weren't put there by any goddamn skookum. There is a chance this man Cayne hasn't shown yet, but by your saying nothing Jack's life could be at risk. You want to settle for that by not telling me?'

Connie hesitated a moment. 'He's riding south to the stage station . . . going to my father's ranch.'

'The Nogales coach?'

'Yes. Aqua Cajon,' she said after a moment's thought.

The lawman gave a brisk *Thank you*, returned to the main street and the nearest open cantina.

He took a quick glance around the single room bar, immediately saw the lone figure of Magro slumped at a corner table. His deputy had his eyes closed, was sitting snoring with many empty tequila glasses in front of him. The lawman shook his head understandingly, went straight on to the lodging house near the centre of the small town.

'Is Señor Luna in his room?' he asked the patron.

'It's the middle of the night,' the man replied unhelpfully.

Rebo looked ominously around him. He noticed the man sitting sprawled in a chair with a range hat covering his face, apparently asleep.

'Is Señor Luna in his room?' he asked for a second and clearly final time.

'*Sí*. A half-hour ago. I think maybe he was *poco* drunk.'

Have you got a sheet of paper . . . a

pen?' Rebo asked.

The man rummaged around under a makeshift desk, produced an old Wanted dodger and a stubby pencil.

'I've got this,' he offered.

Rebo folded the paper and wrote a few words on the back. It was a note for Rafael, saying where he was going.

'Make sure Luna gets this,' he told the patron. Without looking back he walked out to the street, briskly on to the stable to collect his horse.

As soon as Rebo had left the lodging house, the slumping man pulled his hat away from his face. He got to his feet, with his right hand reached behind his back.

A moment later, the surprised patron watched helpless as the point of a skinning knife was jabbed five or six times against his stomach.

'Don't shout. Just keep quiet,' the man warned.

'That's what I'm good at,' the wretched patron mumbled. 'Please don't hurt me.'

'I'm not goin' to do it now. But unless you stay shtum for at least ten minutes, I'll find a way later. *Comprendes?*'

The terrified patron stayed rooted to the spot. Only his eyes moved, rolling around as he listened for any sound from the street. After more than double the ten minutes he dared to move, looked around to see that the man had taken the message intended for Rafael Luna.

6

Muttering aggravations to himself Carlos Rebo led his sorrel into the deserted street. He swung up to the saddle, heeled the animal into a brisk trot towards the shadows of the cedar brake. Despite hot days, border nights were often bitterly cold and he shivered under his mackinaw coat. A nightjar's squawk made him flinch, reminding him of another bird's call when, in the previous year, he'd been shown the body of Will Morgan. For a brief moment he thought the man's features had, in a strange way, resembled those of Jack Finch.

Rebo emerged into the silvery light beyond the brake, set his mount to a canter. He was now thinking seriously about the killer he'd trailed from San Simon. He'd started with a basic description, but since meeting Jack

Finch he knew a bit more how to describe Dawson Cayne. What he and Jack didn't know or understand was the man's reason for murder. Being deluded or psychotic didn't somehow fit.

Three miles from town Rebo could just discern where the south trail ran alongside the deeper shadow of a rimrock ridge. The moon dipped behind the north rim and the lawman slowed his horse, walked it close to the clefted wall. He'd gone about halfway along the section when he stopped.

He swung the sorrel around, peering carefully into the darkness ahead and above. A sense of danger filled the night air and he reached for the butt of his Colt. He was considering the error he might have made when a bright flame stabbed the darkness. An explosion reverberated wildly along the ridge and the first bullet knocked him from the saddle.

You don't need a goddamn cannon from thirty feet, he was thinking

66

ruefully as he hit the ground. Gasping and grinding his teeth at the pain, he was almost up on his knees when the second bullet hammered him between the shoulder blades. Slammed back down with his face twisting against the acrid dirt, he heard a guttural cough from close behind. Then there was deep pain. Then there was nothing.

There was little for anyone to see on Dawson Cayne's face. Just a cold smile, and the pale, straggly hair that hung beneath his range hat.

'You'd have done for me,' he grated. 'An' I didn't need your interference.'

★　★　★

Jack rode into the loose spread of half a dozen adobes, dismounting at the one that carried the stage depot sign. He looped his reins to the hitching pole and stepped up to where a lamp oozed light through a glazed front door.

A night duty clerk was bent over a map of Mexico when Jack entered.

'When's the next Nogales stage?' Jack asked him. 'I want to go to Aqua Cajon.'

The old man looked up and blinked vacantly, but someone else laughed from a dim corner of the room. Jack looked towards the man who rose from a bench seat, stretching his arms in a long yawn.

'Aqua Cajon's a funny sort of place, is it?' Jack retorted.

The big, heavily built man slowly lowered his arms and stared back at Jack.

'Sorry, feller, it's not that,' he said with a smile. 'It's just that we gringos always assume everyone speaks English, no matter what godforsaken world we fetch up in.' The man stepped forward and extended a beefy hand. 'I'm Tolliver Spatch.'

Jack accepted the handshake but didn't give his name. 'I wanted to know about the stagecoach,' he said.

'It's always on time, if that's what you mean. But that means any time between now an' midday,' Spatch said. 'I'll be goin' to Vaca Pasada . . sure be glad o' your company.'

The ride had made Jack tired and achy but he kept the exhaustion hidden behind a straight face.

'Where do you buy tickets?' he asked.

'At this time o' night you pay the driver. This old galoot don't want to keep any money around the place.'

It was cold in the depot, and Jack didn't think anyone would object if he tipped what looked like cow dung and brushwood from a box into the grate. He stirred the lifeless fire to get a flame moving; hunching down he warmed his hands, stared into the gather of yellow flames.

'Well, it's a long haul to reach where you're goin',' Spatch said, settling back down on the bench.

'How do you mean?' Jack asked.

'Aqua Cajon must be at least sixty miles. What's out there that's so important?'

'Just personal stuff,' Jack said without

taking his eyes off the rising flames. 'How about you and Vaca Patata?'

'Vaca Pasada. It's Vaca Pasada,' Spatch corrected, sounding curiously hurt. 'I got me some land. It's a small spread, but the dollars I paid wouldn't have bought a corn crib where I come from.'

'Cattle?'

'Yeah. I'm thinkin' of introducin' some new stock. Build a herd that's small on grass an' big on lard.' Spatch laughed then fixed his eyes on Jack. 'You know anythin' of cattle dealin'?'

'Not much,' Jack lied.

'Hmm. Aqua Cajon, eh?'

'That's what I said.' Jack gave a short nod.

'I guess you must know Ralph Kettle then. Apart from his foreman an' a few cowhands he's the only American out that way. You can see his RK brand in the stockyards all along the border. South of it, that is.'

Jack was aware of the name Kettle, the man he was intending to work for:

Connie's father.

'Why are there so few of us Americans down here?' Jack asked.

Spatch considered his answer for a moment.

'Plenty o' reasons I guess. With the price o' land I couldn't make it anywhere else but Mexico. South of Nogales there's little stomach for business, an' as for the Mexicans themselves, they've got beef comin' out o' their asses. But they hate it. They mix it with chili an' pretend it's somethin' else. So people like me see the gain in movin' it all north to Abilene or Cheyenne.'

'And you all think like that?'

'The few of us who's here, yeah. Except your friend Ralph, o' course. He had another reason, didn't he?'

'I don't know. I've never met anyone named Ralph, Kettle or otherwise.' It was the truth that Jack stated and he turned to stare up at the big man. Spatch grinned.

'If you say so. Perhaps it's just as

well. But as I was sayin', he came south 'cause o' some trouble up near Flagstaff. He crossed half the Colorado Plateau with his whole family in tow. They say his wife originally came from San Miguel.'

That would explain Connie's looks, Jack immediately thought.

'How long ago was that?' he asked.

'About ten years. He might have fled Flagstaff but, as the sayin' goes: 'good luck often comes behind the bad'.'

'It's not inevitable,' Jack said, thinking it must be very difficult and dangerous going forward while looking behind you. There had to be a moment in between. He thought about Connie's lucky acorn in his pocket, sensing he was getting close to needing some of its power. He slowly pushed himself upright, felt weariness taking its toll again. His neck and arm ached, his whole upper body. He stood leaning against the door jamb, gazed into the darkness along the street.

A lone rider was moving in from the

north, appearing gradually through the darkness. Aches and pains momentarily forgotten, Jack felt his muscles tense as the rider came slowly towards him. His mouth turned dry, but the fingers of his right hand flexed as they touched the handle of his Colt.

As the distance closed Jack saw the unmistakable form of a Mexican vaquero. He lifted his left hand, touched the brim of his hat.

'Good evening,' he said.

'Good evening to you,' the rider returned as he swung down and tied his horse alongside Jack's chestnut gelding. 'I'm after the Nogales mail coach — hoping not to be too late,' he added, walking up the steps.

'It's difficult to be that. But there's a fire inside,' Jack offered.

A moment later he turned his back on the street. He could hear the big voice of Tolliver Spatch, plying the newcomer with questions.

'You sure you ain't got a bag o' samples outside, feller?' the man was saying. 'I hear our juice is sellin' real well in your neck o' the woods. No? Well if you really are headed for the RK you won't find it any clambake. Ol' Ralph himself ain't so bad, but his foreman, John Fishback's as mean as a bitin' boar. You'll find out soon enough, though; don't have to take my word for it.'

'I won't, señor,' replied the man who had introduced himself as Raul Chama. 'And as yet, there's no reason for me to get bit.'

Ha! Good for you, Jack thought.

'I'm just givin' you a friendly warnin', feller. Just passin' on what I heard. Apparently there's always an empty bunk at the RK. Fishback works the men 'til they crawl willin' into their crate. Some reckon he's even got a cinch ring on the boss.'

Raul Chama didn't say any more. No one bothered to feed the fire again or stoke the ashes. Jack was thoughtful, troubled by what Spatch had to say about Connie's father. The night clerk went back to studying his maps, taking an occasional look at his stemwinder.

* * *

A north-westerly wind had blown in and dust was swirling around them as they tied their mounts to the rear of the coach, slung their saddles up into the box.

The clerk was standing in the doorway, waited to raise a hand as the coach pulled away, minutes later.

'Back to his maps I suppose,' Raul Chama said, looking back. 'What's to learn about this place? There's nothing but sand in every direction.'

'Yeah, an' then some,' said Spatch gruffly. The wind was insidious, taking all the good-humoured bluff and bluster from him. 'Pull down those goddamn flaps before we choke to death,' he said to Chama while fastening the one on his side of the coach.

With all the flaps now covering the

windows the coach's interior turned gloomy.

'So we catch up on our slumber,' Chama suggested. 'Unless anyone's got something better in mind, I'll be saying *adios*.'

The coach swayed gently across the flat terrain in the cradle of its long, leather thoroughbraces. Settling back in his corner, Jack moved into comfort, then on into sleep.

Hours later he became aware of the change in the light. The window blinds were rolled back up; to the east the sky was streaked with watery colours of dawn. Sitting opposite, Chama was watching him and grinning.

'You had a good sleep, *amigo*,' he said.

Jack flexed his neck, rolled his shoulders.

'I must have needed it,' he replied, feeling a good deal better than he had the previous night. 'Where's Spatch?' he asked quickly.

'He left us about an hour ago. You

miss him already?'

'Yeah, like a rotten molar,' Jack said. 'I'm travelling to the RK as well,' he continued a moment later. 'Thanks for not asking, but I did realize we were going to fetch up there together. I just didn't want ol' trumpet-mouth knowing about it.'

'I understand, *amigo*. And I didn't ask, because we are so close to the border. Such questions are often *imprudente* — unwise.'

'Hmm, I'll remember that,' Jack said. 'How much longer, do you reckon?'

'An hour or so. Looks like we're chasing the rain to get there.'

'Rain?'

'Yes, it does happen. From where I'm sitting I can see it rolling up from the south.'

7

The rain fell steadily. Thin surface mud sucked at the boots of Jack and Raul Chama as they walked the short distance from the coach to the steps of the simply signed Cantina.

'There will only be one of everything, so why name them?' Chama said wistfully. 'Did you see the town notice?' he asked. Jack gave a half-smile.

'I saw it,' he said. 'You and me are pushing the population to over two hundred.'

The interior of the cantina saloon was low on fancy trimmings but high on basic sounds and pungent aromas.

'Come far?' the inscrutable barkeep asked.

'Far enough.' Chama laughed. 'I can see how Aqua Cajon got half its name. Salud,' he said and raised his stubby glass.

One or two bleary-eyed customers looked up, gave a cursory glances towards the two strangers. A tall lean American who was drinking alone at the end of the bar was taking a little more interest.

Jack nodded. 'I'm guessing you're John Fishback,' he said.

'An' I'm guessin' you're Finch an' your friend here's Chama,' the man replied. 'The two hands Mr Kettle's been expectin'.'

Jack gave a faint shrug.

'More or less,' he agreed uncertainly. He couldn't help wondering why Connie hadn't mentioned Fishback, a man who apparently carried some notoriety. Perhaps that's why, he thought. Fishback had an inch or so on Jack, looked like he'd be a tough proposition in a brawl, but his face lacked character. There was fierceness in his stare, but no real steel.

'Let me pay for those dust-cutters,' Fishback said, moving towards them. There was a distinct slur in his voice.

Probably been here all day and all night, Jack thought; didn't say as much.

'No thanks. Being in your debt don't seem the right place to start,' he said.

Going with the sentiment, Chama shook his head.

'We have to see to our horses,' Jack said, intending that Fishback could take it as an excuse. 'They're needing grain and a stall.'

'Suit yourself. When you're done, come back,' Fishback suggested. 'But don't take too long. There's a ranch waitin' for us.'

Jack met Fishback's pale, challenging eyes.

'If you're gone, you're gone. Don't hang around on our account,' he said. 'We'll find our way.' Still looking at Fishback he drained his glass, set it on the bar with a purposeful clunk. Then he placed a dollar coin beside it. 'Give Mr Fishback a drink,' he said quietly. 'It's a private joke. He'll understand.'

Jack followed Chama back out into

the rain. They unhitched their sodden mounts from the rear of the stagecoach, led them into gloom of a livery stable along the street.

A efficient-looking liveryman promised he'd take good care of the horses for fifty pesos. Chama stood watching the man remove the damp bridle and reins.

'I didn't warm to that hombre,' he said to Jack. 'Do you think buying us a drink, was buying us into trouble?'

'Yeah, a first payment. Balance for sometime later, when it better suits him. He's trouble with a kind face.'

'A kind face?' Chama repeated dubiously.

'Yeah, the kind you want to bury your fist in,' Jack said with a cold smile. He handed the liveryman two dollars. 'That's fifty pesos, right?'

'But I didn't come looking for a fight,' he said, turning back to Chama.

Chama smiled. 'Me neither, *amigo*.'

John Fishback wasn't in the cantina when they got back. The bartender pushed Jack's dollar across the counter top.

'Señor Fishback turned you down. Said it was very funny but he didn't want a drink.'

'What else did he say?' Jack asked.

'You can spend the night in town. But to be at the ranch at sunup. He'll be waiting for you.'

'I don't like the idea of keeping someone waiting,' Chama said. 'You got somewhere we can stay?'

The bartender thought for a moment, shook his head as if considering.

'Sorry, señor. We have rooms, but right now they are all occupied.'

Jack gave a derisive look to the floor, the walls around them.

'That's not real easy to believe, mister,' he said. 'Sounds like something Mr Fishback might have said, in view of him being real funny and all.'

'So where would you recommend we bed down?' Chama asked.

The Mexican shrugged uneasily.

'This is the only place, I could recommend, *señor*. But as I said . . . '

'Yeah, I know, you're full to busting,' Jack cut in. The shambling figure of the coach driver rose from a corner table.

'The goddamn coach is free. Take it for another night, why don't you?' he offered. 'It'll be more comfortable, an' a hell of a lot sweeter-smellin'. I ain't goin' anywhere in this weather.'

Jack thanked him. 'A port in a storm, eh? I've spent nights in worse places,' he said.

'If you're workin' for that turkey-cock who was in here earlier, you might be goin' back to one o' them worse places. I wish you both luck.'

'We'll be working for Ralph Kettle, no straw boss,' Jack advised the driver. 'I hope all of your guests haven't eaten all of the food,' he added, turning his eyes on the barkeep.

'Beans an' tomato or beans an' meat,' the barkeep offered.

'I'll take both,' Jack said.

'Me too,' Chama accepted.

'Make that three plates an' three whiskeys. American whiskey,' the coach driver called.

The rain didn't stop. Long after Chama began snoring, Jack was listening to it drumming on the coach roof. He was tired, but his mind was racing. Once again, he saw in his mind's eye things he didn't want to see.

To deaden his aches he'd bought a half-bottle of aguardiente from the barkeep. He took another pull, then settled his head back against the threadbare upholstery, letting the raw, fiery spirit do its work.

* * *

At the first hint of daylight the two men were riding a narrow trail that wound through a thick stand of live oaks, climbing into the northern foothills of the Sierra Madres. Unexpectedly, they rode up to the outer boundaries of the RK ranch. As they crested a rolling hill, they found themselves facing wire.

'Hog-wire. Very nasty,' Jack said. 'No one ever told me they had that down here. I thought it was a ranch we've been riding to, not a farm.'

Reining in, they sat in the predawn light, scanned the flat-roofed adobe buildings nestling beneath the timber-line of the soaring mountain range. Cattle were all over the grass-rich land, and in a corral Jack saw a score of fine horses cavorting about. In the home yard there were a lot of cowboys busy saddling up. The long, low bunkhouse was in the usual place, next to the main house. Yellow light spilled from its open doorway, smoke curled thickly from the chimney.

Chama grinned. 'This is it, *amigo*. At last we've arrived.'

'Not exactly,' Jack said. 'There must be a break along here somewhere.'

They rode along the wire until they came to a gateway with a poker-worked sign.

'RK,' Jack read as he rode through. 'Let's find Fishback.'

Ten minutes later Jack tied his sorrel to the long hitching pole alongside the bunkhouse. He looked straight towards the bulky man who had stepped out to meet them.

'Good morning. We're looking for John Fishback,' he said.

'Morning. He'll be wherever he fell, I expect,' the American answered. 'He certainly tied one on last night; must've drunk the place dry. With you fellers, was he?'

'Not for long,' Jack replied. 'Where can we get coffee?'

'Cookhouse is back o' here.'

Stopping short of a smile, Jack nodded his thanks. With Chama, he walked around to the cookhouse and, with four other shuddering figures, stood around the double-bellied stove. There were three walls, a flat roof and a puncheoned floor on which stood a long table with benches either side.

'I can see why it's tucked away,' Chama remarked. 'For a cowboy drifter, it's not much of an attraction.'

'It weans 'em into what it's goin' to be like for the rest o' the day,' the cook told them. 'They're paid to work, an' breakfast's at five, not mid-mornin'.' He gave Jack and Chama a broad smile. 'Sit yourselves down.'

While the other men joined the group of workers in the yard, the cook filled two tin mugs with strong black coffee, pushed some beans into the direct heat of the stove.

'I'm Hector Bream,' he said, poking the beans with a fork. 'The big barrel you were talkin' to's Walter Bishop. Together with John Fishback an' Kettle himself, we're the only Americans here. Which is OK so long's there's not another goddamn war.'

Like tequila and mescal, the coffee drove away the thought of cold without actually doing much about it. Chama gleefully spooned heaps of sugar from the bowl, and they both tucked away the hot beans. They talked, sat waiting for John Fishback to make an appearance. Most of the hands had ridden out of the yard, and the sun was breaking across the distant mountains before the foreman stepped from the bunkhouse.

Fishback saw Jack and Chama immediately, almost as if he simply wanted to locate them. He ignored them as he passed by, walking on to the corral where a wrangler was breaking out a chestnut gelding.

'He's pretending he doesn't remember,' Jack said to Chama. 'He's one stupid son of a bitch'

'I think he heard you say that,' the young Mexican replied. 'He's coming over.'

Fishback approached the two men, strode through the open front and casually put one boot on the bench next to Chama.

'Well, the pair o' you got here without me,' he ribbed. 'An' breakfast was over an hour ago.'

'*Sí señor*,' Chama replied. 'The cook already told us that.'

Fishback poked a finger into the flesh of Chama's upper arm.

'Now I'm tellin' you. There's a difference.'

Touch me like that if you dare, Jack was thinking. He wondered whether Fishback was a natural bully, or was it race — a people thing? Probably came with being stupid, he decided. A muscle twitched in Chama's jaw.

'*Sí*. There sure is, señor,' he said stiffly.

'Good. An' call me boss,' the foreman said. 'For what remains o' the day you can stay an' help Bream.' That was Fishback's dismissal of Chama, now he turned his glassy stare on Jack. 'Ralph left word he wanted to see you when you arrived, Finch. Sounds like he thinks you're special goods.' The man's body movement inched him towards Jack. 'Is that how you see yourself, feller? Special?' he sneered.

Jack took a deep breath, didn't blink.

'Depends on who I'm next to at the time,' he said. But he was thinking that if Fishback moved an inch nearer he'd smack him one.

Surprised by Jack's reply, Fishback had no quick response. He took his foot from the bench.

'After you've seen Ralph I'll give you chores to put some harder bark on you,' he said.

Jack smiled. 'You don't want to do that, boss, you really don't.'

Fishback was still more taken aback, his face now tinged with concern.

'I was thinkin' you looked kind o' pale, a little doughy,' he said, striding off towards the bunkhouse. 'Let's get movin',' he called back over his shoulder.

Jack caught Chama by the shoulder as the Mexican started after the foreman.

'Steady, *amigo*. You've got the beating of him and he knows it. There'll be a time — believe me.'

'Yes, I know,' Chama said. 'I just wanted to let him know I didn't like him. Nobody's spoken to me like that in a long time. *Un largo tiempo.*'

8

An elderly Mexican answered Jack's knock at the ranchhouse door. He ushered him into the presence of a slight, sharp-featured man seated behind a broad mahogany desk. The man's piercing blue eyes made a quick assessment of Jack, a cautious smile moved his thin lips.

'That's all, Ramon. Thank you,' Ralph Kettle told his house help. He then invited Jack to sit down as the door closed.

Jack sat and stared at his employer. The deep silence was disturbed only by the regular tick of a wall-mounted clock behind the rancher. After thirty seconds Kettle smiled.

'I don't know about you, Mr Finch, but I've been looking for a first impression,' he said. 'I do that for 'most anyone my daughter recommends.'

'I'd say making judgements like that could be a mistake, Mr Kettle,' Jack responded. 'Your daughter recommends many men, does she?' he asked.

'Constanza is forever directing strays this way. It's usually a physical healing of some kind. Some are good — valuable in terms of mutual help — others aren't quite so. My daughter thinks with her heart; an occupational hazard, I guess. Have you eaten?'

'I have yes, thank you.' Jack wondered what sort of healing Connie had in mind for him. 'How do you see me, Mr Kettle? First impressions and all,' he asked.

'Oh, I'm not worried about you,' Kettle said. 'She wrote me . . . touched on your trouble. I appreciate you need somewhere like this where you can regain your strength . . . give yourself time to think.'

'And what do you suppose I'd be thinking about?' Jack asked.

'Probably how to avoid this person who's trying to kill you. The *fusilero*, your friends called him.' Kettle managed to avoid looking directly at Jack.

'I'm not running from anyone,' Jack said.

Now the rancher looked straight at him.

'Are you sure?' he said. 'Are you absolutely sure of that? Constanza wrote me you'd been wounded . . . not too badly but still lucky to be alive. You don't look like the sort of man who fears easily. But you must feel something. An insecurity?'

'Well, I'm not yet recognizing it, Mr Kettle. And I wasn't reckoning on spending more than a couple of weeks here. So, other than the civility of an introduction, was there something else you wanted to see me about?'

'I already said: to give me an impression. For my daughter's sake as well as mine. I accept your motives are your own business, but as long as you're on my ranch I have a vested interest in your welfare. Perhaps even accountable. I'm sure you'll understand, Mr Finch.'

'Sure. Sure I do.'

'Good. And you're welcome to remain here as long as you want. We don't expect you to go bull-running, but you're obviously well enough for lighter chores.'

Jack nodded and stood up.

'Oh, I'm good for those,' he agreed.

'John Fishback will see you get settled in. Feel free to call on me any time,' the rancher said, ushering Jack through the door.

Standing on the wide veranda outside the front door of the house, Jack took a thoughtful look around him. He understood how a scared man might judge another by his own feelings. Perhaps the old rancher wanted a counterpart. If you can't beat someone on your own, seek out a partner with a similar problem. Yeah, that would be it, he was thinking — had nearly said aloud — when the door opened behind him.

'A moment. I should have mentioned that I had a letter from Constanza,' Kettle said, lifting an envelope in his hand. 'She'll be arriving next week. She has a short vacation owing. I thought you'd like to know.'

For Jack, the little twist of pleasure was lessened by circumstance.

'Well, I'm sure that's good news for you Mr Kettle,' he replied. 'But I only knew your daughter as a nurse. Nothing more than that.'

'Hmm, just thought I'd say.' Kettle nodded flatly and turned back into the house.

To Jack's right John Fishback lounged against one of the veranda's corner posts. The man thumbed his Stetson further up on his forehead, made a twisted grin.

'So, playin' piggy-in-the-middle with Miss Connie an' her pa, huh?' he said with a smirk. 'Now I know what makes you so special. Well, feller, I'll tell you what I told the pepper gut. It's me who's got intentions in that direction. You understand?'

Jack laughed, mouthed what he thought was a fitting and droll remark.

Pushing away from the stanchion, Fishback paled.

'You sneery at that?'

'Nurse Kettle's probably used to seeing some sad cases, but none of them will likely be in your league, Fishback. And that's a fact.'

Fishback's hand moved threateningly to the revolver belted high on his hip.

'You're making your mistakes real personal. And pulling that Colt could be the biggest,' Jack warned.

Fishback's chest was heaving quickly with the short irate breaths he was taking. His face was twisted in torment.

'Me coming here was her idea,' Jack said. 'It was a healing concern and suited me at the time . . . still does.' It wasn't all exactly true, but Jack thought it expedient. 'You'll bust something, carrying so much bad humour,' he continued. 'Why don't you calm down? Stick to what you're best at.'

Fishback's gaze was now puzzled. He moved his hand away from his Colt, started what he thought to be an appeasing smile.

'Maybe we got off on the wrong foot. I'm willin' to try again if you are. What do you say?' he offered.

'I say it was how you started off, Fishback. I don't care a tinker's cuss either way. It's your move.'

The RK ramrod paused a moment to think.

'Let's get to the bunkhouse . . . start there,' he said.

Jack recalled Tolliver Spatch's insinuation that John Fishback could be ruling the roost over Ralph Kettle. Suddenly, and to Fishback's way of thinking, Jack Finch had spiked his gun.

'This'll be your beddin' ground,' Fishback nodded towards a row of bunks. 'You an' your Mex friend can take the last two. There's bootlockers underneath if you've anything to stow. Most don't'

'Our horses?' Jack enquired.

'Stables are on the far side o' the corral. Saddles an' bits got their pegs in each stall,' the foreman continued. 'Take your sorrel over an' unsaddle him. After that, I'll show you more.'

* * *

Jack hoisted his saddle on to the wall pegs, groaned with exhaustion as he removed the reins and bit from the sorrel. His legs felt weak, his forehead was clammy; he hunkered down in the stall for a moment.

'Should have stayed in the sick bed a few more days,' he muttered, staring at the tremor in his hands.

He cursed, shook himself when he heard the stamp of a horse as it entered the gloomy building.

Two men greeted each other. One was plainly Mexican, the other spoke in a voice Jack thought he recognized.

'*Como esta?*' the Mexican said.

'Fine, Rico, just fine. Have you seen the two new fellers? They've just arrived. One o' mine, one o' yours.'

'*Sí*. But don't worry. They don't

smell like any kind of lawmen to me.'

'Yeah, well they're the ones you got to look out for. We've got to check 'em out, somehow. We can't shift another beeve 'til we know who they are. You handle yours, I'll see our gringo friend.'

Realizing the two men were talking about him and Raul Chama, Jack cursed silently, looking around him for some sort of way out.

'And what if they are not who they say they are?' the Mexican continued.

There was a long, silent moment before the American answered:

'I don't know, Rico. But getting worried might be a good idea.'

'Jack. Jack Finch. What the hell's keepin' you?' Now it was John Fish-back's voice calling from outside the stables.

There was a short scuffle from the gloomy interior before the American answered back.

'What do you want, boss?'

'One o' the new men. He's in there

with his horse. Tell him to get on with it. I haven't got all day.'

Knowing it was the wrong moment to make any sort of sound, Jack thought long, appropriate curses.

'In here? Hell!' The anxiety was plain in the immediate exchange between the American and the Mexican.

Jack eased himself to standing. He edged sideways around the walls of the stalls, away from the voices.

'*Hola*? Someone in here?' the Mexican called out.

Hardly daring to breathe, Jack gripped his Colt. He knew that whatever he did would have to happen within a very few seconds. Moving as quietly as possible away from the sounds of the searching men, he backed up against the rear of the building. Looking to his left and then right for a back door, he saw where a section of panelling had been removed from a back corner of the stables. It was to allow access to the water barrel from inside as well as out, and there was enough room for him to squeeze through.

He turned, squinting against the light, made a grab for his Colt when he saw the figure directly in front of him.

'*Amigo*. What's wrong?' Raul Chama asked.

Shaking his head and holding a finger across his lips, Jack stepped forward. He led, half-pushed Chama to the frame of a broken calf wagon. Crouching down, regaining his breath, he described what he'd overheard from the stables.

'I can guess what's going on here,' Chama replied. 'There's at least two of them running ahead of any tally. They're working the RK stock. What other reason would there be for them to be out here?'

'You tell me, Raul,' Jack said. 'But if that is what's going on, and those two think I overheard them, they'll want to do something about it.'

'Then you have to convince them you heard nothing.'

'And how do I do that without them not getting suspicious?'

'Pretend you weren't there — that you had left the stables before they arrived.'

A minute or so later Jack circled back around the barn. The corral with its horses gave further cover, from which he emerged when Fishback had his back to him.

'I'm coming. I heard you the first time,' he said, when the foreman called his name again. 'And I told you you'd bust a gut if you carried on like that.'

Fishback looked hard at him for a second, then called out:

'It's all right fellers. I've got him. He's out here.'

'You've got some horseflesh in there. One or two I wouldn't mind myself,' Jack said in support of his deception.

Two men walked side by side from the livery stables; one was a big, hirsute Mexican as tall as Fishback, and the burly man whose voice Jack had recognized: Walter Bishop. They both eyed him with obvious concern.

'So, you got your sorrel settled in?' Fishback asked.

'Yeah, I've done that.'

'Then took yourself a stroll,' Fishback added derisively. He looked towards the surrounding foothills and paused for thought. 'I've got me some business in town today, Walt. Will you show our Mr Finch here around?' he said.

'Yeah, sure thing.' In a low voice Bishop said something to the Mexican, then sidled up to Jack with a smile on his heavy face. 'Until you know the run o' the place, we'll take a buggy,' he said.

Jack nodded and followed Bishop to where a buggy was parked alongside the ranch house. When Bream unhitched the chestnut mare Jack looked back, saw Fishback in close conversation with the Mexican. As Bishop swung the buggy from the yard, the two men gave Jack a look that left no doubt it was him they were talking about.

9

Jack sat awkwardly beside Walter Bishop's bulk as the buggy bounded over the rutted trail. The heavy profile of Bishop gave little hint of what went on in the thick head. But Jack thought there was a slight smirk on the man's lips.

On reaching the RK gateway Bishop swerved the buggy broadside on to the barbwire fence. The manoeuvre almost threw Jack from the seat. He clung on as the guffawing driver whipped the horse to a full gallop through the drifted mesquite and tumbleweed. The lightweight vehicle bucked and bounced. Bishop's eyes rolled, and his coloured teeth fronted soundless laughter.

'You soiled yourself, feller?' he shouted into the turmoil.

'It's getting that way.' Jack gripped

the railing tighter.

Reaching the top of a long, sloping rise, Bishop continued to slap the horse viciously with the reins. Snorting its alarm, the beast surged on. At a breakneck run it was almost dragging the buggy free of its shaft straps. Bishop was holding the vehicle so close to the wire that the wheel hubs on Jack's side scraped the arrow barbs several times.

Suddenly Bishop kicked on the brake and dragged on the reins. The buggy skewed to a sliding halt, the locked wheels steering into clumps of softer ground and grass. Bishop was grinning breathlessly.

'What did you think o' that?' he gasped, turning in the seat.

Jack drew a deep breath, whirled his left fist hard into the smirking features.

Bishop's head didn't move much on its thick neck, but the man rose from his seat, nearly standing, as bright blood dribbled from his mouth. In a short movement Jack drove his right fist low and deep into his back. Bishop's legs weakened, giving way, and he went down, crumpling heavily on to the grass.

'I think you should ask the horse. You're down there with it,' Jack rasped in reply.

The beefy man wobbled to his feet, rubbed his knuckles across his bleeding mouth. He spat, his small eyes filling with resentment.

'You hit me — punched me twice,' he spluttered, his right hand twitching close to his Colt. But something in Jack's angry, challenging gaze warned him, and his podgy-fingered hand drew away.

'One from me and one from the mare,' Jack returned. 'Any more and I'll put you between the shafts. Now get back up here and show me the spread.'

Bishop grasped the railing and swung his weight back into the seat.

'Takes some muscle to put me down, feller,' he puffed, kicking off the brake and taking up the reins. 'We heard you was an invalid, like an outpatient.'

'Who said that?' Jack asked.

'John Fishback said it. So who the hell are you?' Bishop inched away, almost cringing at his own question.

'Who the hell do you think I am?'

'Lawman o' some sort?'

Jack smiled dully. 'I can guess that's what you'd be thinking. But, no I'm not, and I didn't come here looking for trouble. You and your friends can go on shifting beeves.'

'Christ! You heard me an' Rico, talkin'. You were in the stables?'

'Yes I was, you fat thieving son of a bitch.' Jack took a closer look at Bishop 'I might not be after trouble, but I won't be watching you rob Ralph Kettle blind, either. You understand?'

Bishop narrowed his eyes in thought. 'Meanin' what, exactly?'

'You stop what you're doing until I'm gone.'

'You an' your partner? Raul Chama?'

'He's not my partner. We just arrived together.'

'Hmm. We'll take a look at the west

pastures,' Bishop replied, starting to consider Jack's proposal.

Confident that he had Bishop's measure, Jack eased himself into a more comfortable position, thought he'd take in the features and quality of Ralph Kettle's ranch. He saw enough to convince himself it was no shirt-tail outfit. There were at least two thousand head and some of the finest grazing west of the Rio Grande.

Approaching the home yard, Bishop came out with a few more words.

'How long do you figure on stayin' around?' he asked, revealing his real concern.

'Ten days. Three weeks at most,' Jack said as he jumped to the ground. He paused and stared up at the man. 'Is Fishback in on the deal?'

The tip of Bishop's tongue examined his split lip.

'It's just me an' Rico.'

'OK Well, what do you say?' Jack said.

'Two weeks,' Bishop snapped back as

he wheeled away.

Jack watched him walk the buggy towards the livery stables, heard him curse in predictable surprise when Rico seemingly appeared from nowhere to meet him.

At the cookhouse Hector Bream was sitting at the end of the long table, peeling onions.

'Me and Walter Bishop have been getting acquainted,' Jack said. 'Hell, he sure knows how to handle a rig. Have you seen Raul?' he added, pouring coffee from one of the stove pots.

'In the bunkhouse.'

'Thanks.'

Raul Chama shook his head when Jack entered.

'Look. This is the work they expect me to be doing,' he said, pointing to a barrel containing various brooms and brushes.

Jack smiled. 'Yeah, you'd think they'd at least give you a decent mop,' he ribbed. 'But never mind that, just listen to this.' After he'd informed Chama of the morning's events and the deal he'd made with Walter Bishop, the young Mexican's face was even more despondent.

'If they accept that easy, it could be they will put you away,' he suggested. Jack shook his head.

'I don't think so, Raul. Not unless that Rico character's got a lot more grit than Walter Bishop. Besides, I said that killing me would be no good, I'd told you everything. I figure they'll sit tight for a couple of weeks.'

'You do not think it's life or death for them?'

'No, not yet anyways. They can't be rustling on a scale for Kettle to notice. Not unless Bishop lied about Fishback not being in on it. If they wanted to rustle big time, they'd need him. Without him there'd be no way the beeves wouldn't be missed.'

'That's true, *amigo*. But whether he's in or out makes it bad for us.'

Jack smiled again. 'Bad for me,' he corrected. 'I was ribbing you, Raul. I told the fatman Bishop you and me weren't even friends.'

* * *

North Mexico was a deceiving land. A hot, sultry day became a cool afternoon, a sharp, cold night. The sky changed from clear blue to near indigo, and when the sun sank red behind the Sierra Madres a man could be chilled to the bone.

Under the tin roof of the RK cookhouse Hector Bream had stoked his double-bellied stove until it glowed with the heat.

Throughout the meal Rico constantly lifted his eyes to watch Jack. Platters of beans and potatoes and slices of beef disappeared quickly before the keen appetites of the men. Pouring coffee for himself and Chama, Jack listened to the good humour around him. Most of the talk was in Spanish and broken English, but the camaraderie was obvious. And why not? he thought, noticing that

Walter Bishop and Rico hardly joined in.

Rico's dark eyes burned with hostility.

'Hey, gringo,' he called.

In the ensuing silence the crack and spit of logs in the big stove suddenly became the only real sound.

'Hey, I'm talkin' to you, gringo,' Rico called out again.

Jack knew the big Mexican meant him. He placed his mug carefully back on the table in front of him.

'What is it?' he asked, his voice sounding a wearisome edge. Rico stood up and grinned.

'I'm thinking of taking me some exercise,' he said.

'Yeah, you look like you could do with it. What's it got to do with me?'

'It's with your head and your ass I'll be taking it.'

Walter Bishop licked his lips. His flabby face was puffed up with anticipation and his eyes were gleaming. Jack could see it was the grudge he was nursing, and understood the plan. Well, if Bishop had Rico to square things up for him, Jack wasn't about to disappoint.

'There'll be none o' your brawlin' here,' Hector Bream shouted, brandishing a long-handled hot skillet.

Rico beckoned Jack to follow him outside. Raul Chama got to his feet, his expression shouting for Jack not to follow. Common sense told Jack not to go either, but he knew it would only delay the inevitable. Looking into the darkness he recalled a wheatfield and a wind that stirred the calico dress of his dead wife.

'Yeah, let's get on with it, you scrub pig,' he muttered.

Rico was standing a little away from the cookhouse where there was just enough light to see. The Mexican undid his gunbelt. Jack did the same, then turned to Chama.

'No offence, Raul, but no one more than you knows what these goddamn Mexes are like,' he said. 'They're real tricky sons of bitches. If by chance he beats me, shoot him dead. Then Bishop. Then ride back to civilization.'

From the open-ended cookhouse the punchers watched as Rico stepped a couple of paces to Jack's right, then back to the left. He was grinning, sizing Jack up.

'So, gringo man, I am not as fat or as slow as Walter Bishop,' he hissed unpleasantly.

'No, you're more like a big monkey,' Jack said, remaining very still.

Dropping his left shoulder, Rico took a quick step forward. He crossed the knuckles of his right fist across Jack's jaw. Shaking his head at the small, dancing stars, Jack hopped out of the reach of Rico's long arms. The Mexican had fists like rocks; if he made a wrong move it would be like being kicked by a balky horse, probably bringing terminal injury.

His senses clearing, Jack took Rico's next barrage head on. He managed to block most of the blows on his shoulders and forearms. He threw a punch up to the broad forehead, saw an instant look of shock in the man's savage eyes. But it wasn't near enough to stop or slow Rico down; he went on swinging heavy punches, grunting with lust and exertion. They were all numbing blows and Jack was beginning to tire.

A pistoning fist thudded into Jack's ribs, driving the breath from him. Trying to smother the brutal onslaught, he made a grab for Rico. He stumbled, and Rico brought a knee up. Jack gasped with pain and, dropping his arms, staggered backwards. He was trying to retreat from the man's range, but a set of hard knuckles battered the side of his face.

Jack could hear Raul Chama's shouting protest as he rolled on his back. On the hard-packed dirt, for a few seconds he wallowed in a blaze of pain. Then Rico was there with his boot raised.

There was a shout for Rico to stop,

and the Mexican hesitated. But someone else intervened, louder than the
others:

'Let 'em fight.'

Jack turned his head, focused on the
tall figure of John Fishback staring
down at him.

'We get little entertainment as it is.
Let 'em fight,' the foreman repeated, an
eager grin across his face.

Rico needed only Fishback's OK to
drive his boot down on Jack's face. But
Jack had used the few seconds of respite
and was ready. As the boot came down
he grabbed at Rico's ankle with both
hands, pulled and twisted in one
desperate movement. Rico went over
and down, sprawling heavily on his
face. Jack pushed himself to his knees,
grabbed a fistful of Rico's greasy black
hair and pulled his head up.

He drove in three chopping blows,
each more powerful than the last,
before letting go of Rico's head. He
took in a gulp of air, felt a hand grip his
shoulder.

'You've beat him,' Fishback said. 'An' ol' Ralph implied you were next to crow bait.'

'It's a matter of timing.' Jack was too winded to say more. Too dry to spit at the ground.

Chama stepped in. He picked up Jack's gunbelt and helped him to the bunkhouse.

'That son of a bitch wanted Rico to dance on my head,' Jack groaned as he rolled on his bunk. 'He's got to be working with them — Bishop and Rico.' Jack cursed and ground his teeth against the pain. 'They figured Rico would do me serious harm — probably kill me in a fight. It would look like another tolerable loss for the ranch.'

Chama gave a sombre nod.

'Maybe we should leave this place, *amigo*. The money either of us gets isn't enough for this. It's not what I was expecting.'

'Nor me,' Jack agreed. 'And to think it came recommended. I've a bone to pick with young Connie when she gets here. As for her pa's cowboys and their rustling, at the moment it's only our word against theirs.'

Chama fetched a water dipper, handed it to Jack.

'I don't want to stay here if it's just to get some proof. It's no business of mine, *amigo*,' he offered.

Jack drank the water, handed back the dipper and lay back on the bunk. For more reasons than just finding himself some camouflage or a 'fraidy hole, he'd already decided he was staying. If the fight had been arranged Connie herself might be in some sort of danger. He thought she deserved better than Fishback's fervid intentions.

10

Something awakened Jack before first light. Maybe it was the snoring, or the heavy air of a dozen sleeping men, or the ache low in his belly. Whatever the cause, he couldn't sleep any longer so he got up and dressed. He buckled on his gunbelt, quietly slipped outside and saw that Hector Bream was already busy at his stoves.

'Good morning,' Jack greeted as he entered the open-fronted cookhouse.

Adjusting the dampers, the cook raised a hand and nodded.

'He hurt you, did he, the big Mex?' he mumbled.

'Yeah, but I'll live,' Jack replied. He lifted the coffee pot, saw it held the grounds from the night before.

'When these fires are up an' runnin', I'll make some,' Bream said. 'Hand me some wood, will you?'

Jack gave him brushwood from a box as he needed it. The fires took hold and Bream grinned.

'Hah. I never seen this as a two-man business before,' he chuckled. He slammed the stove doors shut, filled a pot and they waited for the water to boil.

'What was your little scrap about last night?' Bream asked.

'You obviously haven't heard the warning about asking questions,' Jack advised.

'It don't include me, feller.' Bream didn't smile. 'Well, you best watch out for that Mex, Rico. He's a mean one. I wouldn't turn my back on 'im.'

The sky above the distant mountains lightened. Jack held his hands over a stove, stomped his feet to get some blood moving.

'I'll remember that,' he said and went outside. He stared thoughtfully at the hand pump for a moment, then spurted cold water over his head. He rinsed his mouth and teeth, turned to the cookhouse and spat. John Fishback had appeared, was standing watching him.

'Hey Champeen,' the foreman greeted. 'You trainin' for a rematch?'

'No need. Next pigeon's you,' Jack snapped back.

This time Bream did smile and laugh, and Fishback gave him a withering glance.

'Why'd you say that?' Fishback asked.

'You know why. You want me to say in front of your camp cook?'

The foreman watched Bream placing more kindling in the stoves.

'Take a walk, Hec,' he told him. After Bream had strolled across the yard in the direction of the bunkhouse Fishback turned back to Jack.

'Well?' he demanded.

'Dumbness fits your face,' Jack said. 'I'm talking about the little extra cattle business you and Rico and Walter Bream have got going.'

Fishback's mouth opened, twisted into a cynical smile. He shook his head slowly. The foreman's manner didn't make sense to Jack.

'Suppose I ask Ralph Kettle if he ever confirms the tally sheets for range and home pasture with stock pens?'

'You go right ahead an' ask him whatever you like,' Fishback replied. He tested the heat from the coffee pot, immediately shook his burning fingertips. 'You want some o' this?' he asked.

For the shortest moment Jack wondered if Fishback was really in on the deal.

'Yeah, why not? It doesn't mean we're affianced,' he said quietly.

Jack sat down and stared at the table in front of him. What made the ramrod so confident, he wondered. The man should have been in a cold sweat. Instead he looked, sounded like someone holding a full house.

Hector Bream came back to the cookhouse. 'All right if I cook now, boss?' he enquired, eyeing Fishback tetchily.

'Sure, you carry on,' the foreman

replied. 'An' if you don't like the way I run things here, you can leave,' he told Jack. 'The coach that brought you to Aqua Cajon runs the other way.'

'If and when I do leave I'll be ripping a strip off your hide on the way out,' Jack said.

Once again, Fishback appeared to shrink in confidence. His face paled and his Adam's apple danced in his throat.

'What the hell's eatin' you, Finch?' he complained. 'I came down heavy on Rico for starting the brawl.'

'More like gave him different orders and upped his fighting wages,' Jack said and sipped his coffee, saw Bream lighting a couple of brea lamps inside the cookhouse.

'Why did you come here?' Fishback continued. Jack looked down at the mug in his hand.

'Ah, that's for me to know, Fishback. For you to maybe worry about.'

'The way I heard it, you're on the border owl-hoot with a whole passel o' folk after your ass.'

Jack felt his pulse race, the blood rush to his head. Because there was an element of truth in what Fishback said he didn't look up. He knew that if he saw even the hint of a smile on Fishback's face, he'd react. He placed both his hands flat on the table, thought it showed clear meaning.

'I suppose it was Ralph Kettle who told you that, as well?' he suggested.

'Yeah, who else?'

Jack agreed, thought it made some sort of sense. Presumably it was only Kettle himself who knew of Connie's letters. But it was highly unlikely, hard to believe that he discussed such private affairs with his foreman. Now Jack got to wondering about Ralph Kettle as well as Fishback. If Jack was going to stick around there were a few questions he was interested in getting answered.

'I guess everyone's runnin' scared o' someone or somethin',' Fishback taunted.

Jack cursed, got to his feet and

squared up to the foreman. Fishback was surprised and backed off a short pace.

'Best way to get your blood racin', gents,' Hector Bream said, stepping between them. 'But not in my house.'

As if at a timely moment, the ranch's wranglers and punchers were suddenly filing from the bunkhouse, hurrying towards the cookhouse. Jack's temper settled down and he moved to a seat next to Raul Chama.

After breakfast the men got their work assignments. The punchers led their horses into the yard and saddled up, John Fishback told Chama to go with Bishop. He paired Jack with Rico, suggesting they round up strays that had broken through one of the northern fences and were strolling towards the foothills.

'They won't have climbed too high,' he assured them, giving Rico a wink. 'Not above the timber line, anyways. Just find 'em and drive 'em back. *Buena suerte.*' Fishback's last words were larded with mood and definitely for Jack's benefit.

'What's the idea, Fishback?' Jack asked. 'I didn't come here to look for breachy cows.'

'Don't tell me you ain't strong enough to round up a few strays,' Fishback responded. 'If that's the case, I ain't got a use for you. This ain't a greenhorn outfit. If you don't like it see the boss tonight. Meantime get out o' my sight.'

Fishback rasped some unintelligible words, waving at the punchers to mount and get going. Still shouting orders, within seconds he was mixing with the swirls of dust being hoofed into the morning air.

Rico grinned. 'I won't be looking to hurt you, gringo. Not just yet. Let's vamoose,' he said.

Grasping the horn Jack swung into the saddle. In the mix of RK riders he saw Raul Chama astride a remuda mare. Bishop was alongside him on a similar mount. Chama lifted his chin, a restrained sign of assurance he would take due care.

Rico set off around the house, yelling at Jack to follow. Narrow strips of worn trail wound among the green hills, were visible nearly all the way to the timber line. Jack couldn't tell whether it was to or from trouble that Rico was spurring his yellow dun.

* * *

One section of the fence had been breached. While Rico dismounted to look at the ends of the wire Jack traced the tracks of the cattle up the pine-studded slope above them.

'No cow has shoved its way through this,' Rico said. 'The wire's been cut.'

Jack forgot the hostility for a moment. He got down and had a closer look. The Mexican was right, a pair of pliers had been used on the wire.

'What the hell's all this about?' he said, as much to himself as to his harsh-faced companion. Rico peered up at the trail the cattle had chosen.

'I don't know,' he replied. 'Unless it was the phantom cattle thief . . . Cattle Kate.'

'With her wire cutters,' Jack added derisively. 'Maybe your partner's doing some rustling he forgot to tell you and Fishback about.'

Immediately Rico's dark eyes turned hostile.

'You have a big mouth, Finch. I can close it here and now if you want.'

The elemental anger of the big Mexican amused Jack.

'You need to go look in a mirror, Rico,' he said. 'Have you already forgot what happened the last time you tried that? Let's get on with finding the beeves. We can fight in our own time.'

'You mean we don't want Mr Kettle paying for it,' Rico returned. 'OK gringo, lead the way.'

'Yeah, like I'd do that,' Jack told him. 'Get going.'

Rico spurred his horse up the slope and Jack followed. The grade grew steeper and after a while they had to wigwag their mounts for a better footing in the looser ground.

An arduous twenty minutes later, Rico stopped. He pointed ahead and down into a dry gulch.

'*Dios mio*! Look there,' he rasped.

The bottom of the steep-sided gully was choked with pine branches and brush, and, among the mass of fractured timber lay the remains of the strays.

Rico swore. 'They've been run in from above. Straight off the overhang,' he said. 'This isn't rustling, it's murder. *Insano*. Crazy murder.'

Jack remained motionless, gazing down at the eerie carnage below. He shuddered involuntarily when a breeze soughed through the pine that surrounded them.

'We're not driving them anywhere now,' he said. 'Let's turn around.'

'You feel it too?' Rico asked.

'Feel what?'

'Something evil. There's nothing here

. . . nothing living,' the Mexican said, his eyes moving around slowly. 'I'll go and look at those beeves, make sure they're ours. Then we'll go back.'

Jack shaded his eyes against the sunlight and looked up, wondering where the vultures were, whether they would brave the confines of the gulch for meaty spoils.

'Yeah I feel it,' he replied moments later. He watched Rico letting his horse cautiously pick its steps as it descended. He buttoned the neck of his jacket and nudged his gelding on, his right hand resting on the butt of his Colt. When he reached the bottom ground Rico was already amongst the brushwood, counting the dead cattle.

'It's like a goddamn ice house down here,' Jack said, blowing on his hands. The Mexican grunted a reluctant acknowledgement.

'There's six — maybe seven,' he confirmed. 'I'm not going to make sure. But they are RK stock.' He clambered from the tangled crush of timber and glared at Jack. 'Is this to do with you, gringo? You and your greaser friend? Last night when everyone was sleeping?'

'You fool, Rico. You really are more stupid than you look,' Jack retorted. 'You know this was nothing to do with me or Chama. But if Fishback told you to provoke me, there's no need. Just go ahead and pull that Colt you're so fond of touching every few seconds. Go on. Try and shoot me, you poor excuse.'

Rico shook his head. 'Let's just get the hell away from this place.'

Jack guessed the vibrations of voodoo worried Rico far more than any supposed mission to bushwhack him. He dismounted and turned the gelding around, and, holding the reins in his left hand, walked as fast as he could from the gulch, back into the sunshine. After waiting a short while Jack yelled for Rico but there was no answer.

'He can find his own way,' he muttered loudly as he climbed back into the saddle. Then he started down the long stony grade, returning to the RK boundary fence.

Less than five minutes later a single gunshot crashed out and his gelding stumbled and collapsed. He kicked free of the stirrups and jumped clear of the horse as it snorted and squealed to the ground.

'You killed the horse, you son of a bitch,' Jack yelled, rolling into a large clump of white bull-nettle. He twisted his head and saw the gelding's lustrous brown eyes rolling and its chest heaving. He grabbed for his Colt and touched the empty holster, twisted back and saw it lying beside the dying horse.

Back up the grade Rico walked into view. He had his rifle in his hands and, like someone who thought they had downed their quarry, he was on foot.

'Mistake, you cowardly scum,' Jack seethed. He looked at his Colt, then to the gelding whose nose was oozing bright blood. He cursed, lifted himself from the ground cover and stumbled forward on his knees.

Rico fired again and the sound rolled overhead. Dirt erupted in front of Jack's face and he turned and flattened himself amongst more nettle.

The desperation of his plight made Jack's whole body shudder. As the echo died he knew the Mexican was approaching.

'Walk on, Rico,' he shouted. 'Come much closer and I'll put you down again.'

Rico hesitated. He could probably see the dying horse and probably also the wrecked stock of Jack's rifle protruding from the saddle scabbard. But the Colt would be hard to see. He gave a throaty laugh.

'You don't have a gun, gringo.'

'Yeah. And you thought you were going to whup me in a fist fight.' Jack took one look around as if he'd find something else to fight with, then he leapt to his feet. 'Try and hit this,' he dared loudly.

He was up and running hard further down the slope, looking ahead for some sort of cover. He flinched as the next explosion of the rifle rived and pulsed the air around him.

Hell, I'll face him head on, he thought.

Jack stopped in his tracks, turned round to see whether Rico was standing where he'd been a few moments earlier, close to the dead gelding and his .44 Colt. But the Mexican had dropped his rifle, was crumpling, twisting as he fell.

Drawn by incomprehension, Jack went two, then three paces to meet the fallen Rico. He couldn't figure what had happened as his attention locked into the Mexican's contorted features.

Rico's neck muscles flexed. '*Como?*' he gasped, then his eyes closed and his head lolled.

Jack kneeled and grabbed the body. He turned it over away from him, grimaced at the dark blood that stained the back of the cloth chaqueta.

'Wasn't me,' he mumbled, peering at the trees and the rocks above. 'It's someone up there. Whoever pushed those beeves over.'

Jack looked at the gelding, its legs now stiff and unmoving in death. The yellow dun had followed Rico but, unmoved by the gunshots, was now snatching at cholla. Everywhere was suddenly quiet, deathlike quiet.

Jack picked up his Colt, fetched the dun and led it back to Rico. He reholstered the Winchester and heaved the big Mexican up behind the saddle. Sensing that he was being watched, he swung up in front of the body and jabbed his boots in the stirrups. 'Take us back,' he said, lightly heeling the horse's flanks.

I'd have been a dead man if it was meant, he thought as they approached the boundary fence, close to the RK gateway. Then he said aloud, 'Who the hell are you?' looking to the timber line behind him.

The pine-covered slopes were several miles off when he rode into the home yard and drew rein, but he still sensed that he was being watched.

11

Hector Bream came running into the yard when he heard Jack's shout. His features tightened at the sight of Rico draped across the back of the yellow dun.

'What happened? Is he dead?'

'Not yet, I don't think.' Jack quickly started to untie the ropes securing Rico. 'Give me a hand will you?' They lifted the unconscious Mexican and carried him into the bunkhouse. 'Where the hell is everyone?' Jack said.

'Out on the range, where else? Was it you?' the cook asked.

'Shot him?' Jack shook his head. 'Probably the rustlers.'

'Rustlers?' Bream's face contorted with shock. 'What are you talkin' about?'

'Never mind. He needs a doctor and quick.'

Rico made no sound, didn't attempt to move. Jack unbuttoned his jacket, moved his body around and drew the garment off.

'Hell, you can't tell where his flesh ends and his vest begins,' Jack said with distaste. 'The bullet can't have hit anything, but must be goddamn close to his ticker. Do what you can to keep him still while I go for a doc. Don't try to clean him up or use any carbolic. That'll finish him off for sure,' he added and walked outside.

Jack remounted the Mexican's dun and heeled urgently. As he rode from the yard, he saw Ralph Kettle standing on the house veranda. The rancher lifted a hand but Jack didn't respond. There wasn't time and he was beginning to wonder about the old man and his interests.

A wind had got up, was coming in hard and low, rippling the grassy hills. The RK sign over the gateway was swinging and dark clouds were approaching from the south. Deciding to have a look beyond Aqua Cajon, Jack thought wryly. Riding to the small town he saw no one. His mind was racing with questions and answers, the memory of the cattle in the gully, the appalling sense of stealing cattle just to run them over a cliff.

★　★　★

The rain was already falling when he reached town. He quickly located the surgery of Alvaro Lopez, medico, smiling coldly at what Chama had said about there being no need to give the town's cantina a name. He quickly explained the bones of the situation to Lopez.

'He'll probably be dead by the time you get there, Doc, but I'll have tried. I'll get me a drink and follow.'

Jack walked swiftly to the cantina, which was near empty.

'Cheap American whiskey,' he ordered from the inscrutable barkeep.

'How is Señor Fishback treating

you?' the man said as he filled a shot glass.

'Bello. Just bello,' Jack said and swallowed. He stood very still, allowing the fiery liquid to deliver its crude warmth, then he paid, nodded and walked away.

Ducking his head against the wind, he hurried to the livery where the gelding was feeding. The liveryman didn't seem to be around so he placed a short stack of coins on the anvil.

A door creaked from a draught as he found the horse in a rear stall and led it out. For a moment the feeling of being watched returned, as if someone had been standing in the gloom at end of the stables.

'There's money on the anvil. Near enough to fifty pesos, right?' he called out, hoping it might placate a harm-doer in the shadows.

He took a deep breath, waited a moment, then led the horse out front and mounted up.

The windswept rain buffeted him as

he rode down the main street. Passing the saloon he thought he glimpsed the liveryman through the half-open batwing doors. Bewildered, yet glad of the liquor circulating in his blood, he rode beyond the rudimentary town buildings to the north trail. Far ahead, the doctor's horse and buggy were trailing dust.

The buggy was parked in the ranch yard when Jack arrived. A group of saddled range horses were standing about, but the place seemed deserted except for Hector Bream. The man appeared pale, sweaty and tense, as though carrying a big problem.

'You sure as hell made a mistake coming back,' he blurted out. 'They're sayin' you shot Rico.'

'Yeah, I been thinking they might,' Jack replied. 'And bringing him in, then riding to get a doctor — the obvious thing to throw off suspicion. Yeah, predictability's not something they keep hidden. What about you?'

Bream shrugged. 'Walt reckons it.

An' Fishback. If I was you mister, I'd get back on your horse an' ride on.'

'Where is Fishback?'

'They're in the house. They took Rico there a few minutes before the doc got here.'

'And Raul Chama. Where's he?'

Bream shrugged again. 'They thought he was in with you. He's in the bunkhouse.'

Chama lay on his back. His face was puffy, covered in a spread of dark bruises.

'Hey *amigo*.' He managed a ragged smile, moving split lips. 'They didn't think I'd be riding anywhere today.'

Jack helped Chama sit up, swing his legs to the floor and get to his feet.

'We should have left the first day we got here,' the Mexican said. 'Do you remember me saying?'

'Yeah, I remember.'

Chama nodded. 'How do I look?'

'Not pretty. Wait here,' Jack said, striding purposefully towards the bunkhouse door.

'Where are you going?' Chama called.

'Something for John Fishback.' Jack stepped out into the curtain of rain and Chama's protest was immediately lost.

As he walked up the broad front steps of the RK ranch house Jack saw that the front door was slightly ajar. The hall was deserted, but a murmur of voices was coming from beyond the study door. He stepped cautiously across a pair of Navaho rugs and immediately groaned, clamped his jaws when the barrel of a shotgun jabbed at his lower spine.

'Been waitin' for you. Undo your belt an' drop it,' Walter Bishop said.

'Is he dead?' Jack asked.

'Not far from, feller. You want to pray to somebody he stays alive. If he don't, you an' your pard'll join him in the bone yard . . . after swingin' from a rope, that is.'

'Goddamn it, it wasn't me who shot him,' Jack started, and half-turned. He saw a blur of the man's meaty face, the swinging steel of the shotgun barrels. A fateful thought hit him into darkness: the mind-bending idea that Bishop had fired both barrels into his face.

When Jack opened his eyes his face was pressed hard against the floor-boards, up close to the toe end of pair of boots. He swallowed, twisted around and looked up, saw a thin grin appear across Fishback's mouth.

'You're not gettin' up from this,' the foreman threatened.

'Leave him alone,' another voice cut in.

Jack sat up. Through his fogged vision he saw the near-rueful face of Ralph Kettle. He raised his fingers to his forehead, touched the pain spot and looked at the blood on his fingers. He wanted to say that Kettle might have a problem explaining his newly acquired facial damage to Connie when she arrived.

'I wonder if you'd do the same for them,' he offered instead, trying to get up. A dizzy wave of nausea grabbed him and he went back to kneeling.

'I should've fired,' Bishop taunted.

But then another door opened and Doctor Lopez emerged.

'I've done all I can,' he said. 'If he's lucky, he'll live . . . *un invalido*.' He saw Jack on the floor 'Que es? This is the man who came to fetch me.'

'Yeah, that's him,' Fishback said. 'The one who did the shootin'.'

'And he came back? I don't understand.'

'Nor do I,' Kettle said. 'It's got nothing to do with allaying suspicion. The doc's right. Why in God's name would he come back?'

'Suppose we ask Rico?' the foreman suggested.

'Es imposible,' Lopez objected. 'I have taken what must be a big rifle bullet from his back and he is full of morphine. He is very weak and very asleep. But remember, your man Rico would be dead if this man on the floor had not brought him in. *Ciertamente*.'

'I think you're talkin' about Finch

144

bein' innocent until proved guilty,' Fishback said. 'So, we'll try an' forget that last night him an' Rico had a fight; that there's plenty of ill feelin' there. Yeah, that's it. As sure as the sun's now comin' up in the west, we'll believe that some goddamn rustler shot Rico, but decided to let Finch live on. Well, meantime, the turkey's goin' to be trussed up an' watched. Walt, get him out o' my sight.'

Jack waved Bishop away and rose unsteadily to his feet.

'He's hurt,' Lopez said.

'It's just a knock,' Fishback returned.

'Let the doc see his head,' Kettle said.

'Goddamn his head,' the foreman exploded. 'Take him to the stable.'

Jack saw Kettle's authority waver. Walter Bishop laughed and once more prodded his shotgun into Jack's back.

'Hey turkey. Boss said to move,' he said.

Cursing inwardly at Bishop's use of the word 'boss', Jack moved slowly ahead of the shotgun. He knew the fleshy ranch hand didn't have the grit to pull the triggers, unless it was in wretched fear to save his own skin. But if he was prompted by Fishback and a skinful of whiskey, maybe he could fit a noose around someone's neck and smack a horse's rump. There was a difference.

Suddenly Jack caught his breath, but it was in surprise. He'd noticed Chama stealing around the corral; he forced himself to look away, show no notice.

Inside the stable Bishop watched as two Mexican cowhands used hobble strings to tie him to a stall post.

'Come on feller, tell me you shot Rico in the back,' the man rasped. 'Tell me or I'll make *pozole* from your goddamn head.'

'Do it,' Jack replied with a tight, insolent grin. Raul Chama's proximity was his whiskey, his courage from a bottle. 'Even you should be able to handle a man with no arms,' he risked.

Bishop grunted, punched him solidly

between the eyes. Jack's head jerked against his tensed neck and slammed hard against the stall post.

12

The rain spat like hail in the early darkness overhead. Jack's jaw ached and throbbed. Spitting, he turned his head to get some of the stiffness from his neck. Remembering Walter Bishop's blows, he winced again.

'Oye! Bring me some water,' he yelled in the gloom.

For a while no one responded to his calling. Not for the first time since arriving at the RK ranch Jack's mind sped through the why's and wherefore's. Then a shadow moved across the open stable doors.

'Give me some water,' Jack shouted again, but the figure didn't move. 'Whoever you are. I'm not supposed to die of thirst, goddamnit!'

Moments later Jack heard the knock of the pitcher against a barrel, water being poured.

'I can hear you behind me, you son of a bitch,' Jack seethed. 'Let me see you. Give me the water.' Then silence returned and all he could hear was the hammering rain.

Too big for Raul Chama, Jack thought. Maybe it was Hector Bream. So, why the hell didn't he say anything?

A reason for whoever it was having moved quickly on became obvious with the sound of boots slopping through mud and the flash of a lamp. Walter Bishop appeared, his broad, slickered shoulders gleaming in the lantern light.

'Hell of a night,' he moaned. He shrugged off his oilskin and placed a covered platter at Jack's feet. 'It's the grub. Mr Kettle says to feed you. I reckon it's a waste — should be fed to Hec's young wooshers. Why fatten you up to dance at the end of a rope?' Bream's eyes gleamed. 'An' if you're thinkin' Rico's goin' to save you, he ain't. He'll have cashed in before sunup.'

'So, how am I supposed to eat this hog food?'

Bishop dragged his Colt out and pushed the barrel into the middle of Jack's back. He untied the rawhides and Jack vigorously rubbed his wrists.

'You ain't eatin' with your feet,' Bishop said, lifting the platter. 'They stay tied.'

Jack took a bite from a thick biscuit. Scooping a potato up with his fingers he thumbed it into his mouth.

'You've served it without gravy. Now give me a drink,' he said after chewing and swallowing.

'A last request. Why not?' Bishop muttered. He went over to the water barrel, brought the pitcher back and held it just out of Jack's reach.

'I got a gut feeling about you,' Jack said with a smile.

Bishop drew the pitcher further back, pushed his Colt forward.

'What about me?' he asked, frowning.

'I don't think you've got the guts to shoot a man while he's looking at you.

150

Especially when his mouth's full of taters,' Jack said. 'Now I'm going to untie my feet and see if I'm right,' he added, giving Bishop a wink.

'You keep real still,' Bishop threatened. 'I don't have to kill you, just break you up some.'

It was a calculated risk, but right then it seemed it was all Jack had to go on. He put down the platter and started to fiddle with the rawhide knots.

As if to carry out his threat Bishop systematically thumbed back the hammer of his Colt.

Thinking maybe he was mistaken in his opinion of the man, Jack froze at the sound of the dull, ominous click. If Bishop didn't want to displease Fishback maybe he would panic, be capable of some dastardly action. But then, once again, Jack saw the slight figure of Raul Chama stepping out of the rain. He held out his hands and nodded.

'OK. I don't reckon I need any more damage,' he conceded.

The instant relief which washed over

Bishop's big face gave way to alarm when Chama jabbed three or four times into the man's flabby backside.

'Just drop the Colt,' the Mexican said.

The pistol thudded on to the hard-packed dirt of the stable floor and Bishop mumbled something offensive.

Chama removed the pitcher from Bishop's other hand and sent a nervous smile towards Jack.

'Now we vamoose, eh *amigo*?' he said.

Jack untied his feet and ankles, kicked the loops away and took the water pitcher from Chama. He drank its contents all in one long gulp, then tossed the pitcher back towards the barrel.

'Why? I didn't shoot Rico,' he said.

'This fat, trigger-happy crawfish is one reason. He's not interested in whether you are innocent.'

Jack picked up Bishop's Colt and swung it hard across the back of his head.

'So, take your gun back,' he rasped

angrily as the man sank baggily to the ground.

'Now there is another reason, besides Rico,' Chama said anxiously. 'I think we should ride.'

'The fat son of a bitch wanted to shoot me. He was getting ready,' Jack replied. Suddenly he stopped and listened. 'You hear? The others are out front. Quick, kill the light.'

Chama doused the lantern and the stable returned to deep gloom.

'You still in there?' Hector Bream called out.

'You know I am. What do you want?' Jack returned.

'John Fishback an' a few o' the punchers are whiskey mad right now. There's a real lynchy sound to 'em. I come to let you know.'

'Where are they?' Jack asked.

'In the bunkhouse. But not for long. I don't hold with lynchin'. I could get you untied.'

'Someone's already done that,' Jack said. 'Get back to the cookhouse and keep your head down. There'll be some stuff flying around. And thanks.'

Jack and Chama listened carefully as Bream walked away back into the night. In the weak shaft of light spilling from an opening door, they caught sight of him hurrying towards the cookhouse. Through the curtain of rain they also saw a group of men stumbling from the bunkhouse.

'I know a way out. Stay close,' Jack said. It took a minute, but Jack led him to the rear of the building. Chama turned, peered anxiously back into the gloom.

'They won't know about this. Come on,' Jack said. 'At least Bishop won't be following.'

Alongside the rain barrel, which was already near to overflow, the two men squeezed through the loose panels, sliding and stumbling beyond the calf wagon towards a line of outhouses and toolsheds. Jack gripped Chama's arm.

'This is as far as I'm going. I already said why.'

The Mexican pulled Jack's hand away.

'So you stay and die, telling them you didn't do it?'

'You tell me. Do you too think I shot Rico in the back . . . bushwhacked him?' Jack grated. 'Do you think I'd shoot you for knowing, eh?'

'No. Yo no. It doesn't matter what I think,' Chama said miserably.

'*Adios*, Raul,' Jack replied brusquely. 'Come back if you change your mind.'

There were now men with lanterns approaching from between the side of the barn and the corral. The lights wavered, glistening on the patchy grass that surrounded the home yard.

'There's no other way they could've come,' John Fishback shouted.

Jack waited until Chama had disappeared, then he stood quietly in the narrow gap between the outbuildings. He didn't blame Chama for leaving. The man had a life to live, whatever and wherever it was. Grimly he watched the men coming into view. They stood against the rain-streaked beams of light, weaving cautiously from side to side. He recalled something his father had once said about when enemy troops were advancing. If you don't shoot, you won't hit.

He actioned his Colt, stepped forward and fired.

'Get out of the rain, fellers,' he shouted. 'It's not a good place to die, for any of us.'

Three men went silent, stopping in their tracks. The lanterns stopped their searching swing.

'You're the only one goin' to die, Finch. At the end of a rope,' Fishback shouted back.

Taking good steady aim, Jack fired and smashed out the lantern nearest to him. Then he moved, using the outhouses as cover and walked fast towards the lights of the main house.

Flame gashed the darkness behind him. Two men were shooting blind, the third was showered with glass shards and flaming gobbets of oil. Taking the broad veranda steps two at time, Jack pressed his back to the wall alongside one of the windows that flanked the front door.

'You might be the only ally I've got now. Where the hell are you?' he muttered.

Jack looked down at his feet. The water dripping from the brim of his hat formed a dark stain around the toes of his boots. He was cursing silently, thinking of how he might settle things, when the window frame scraped noisily as it was lifted open.

A shadow was cast down on to the veranda floorboards and Ralph Kettle was calling from inside.

'What's the shooting? What the hell's going on?'

Cold sweat trickled down Jack's face as his assailants approached the house and came up the steps. He raised his Colt, held it flat across his chest.

'John? What's happened? I heard a shot,' Kettle called out again.

The men were in a quandary. They

could see Jack standing on the far side of the window, just as he could see them.

'Ralph, get your head in. There's goin' to be more shootin',' Fishback responded.

Getting the gist of a meaning, Kettle turned to see Jack only a few feet away. 'No,' he yelled. 'Rico isn't dead yet. That saddle-bag doctor's saved him. He's pulling through . . . going to live.'

Ah good, I'm so goddamn pleased, Jack thought bitterly. He fought away the image of Annie, her calico dress and the waves of yellow corn.

13

Rico's dark eyes had lost some of their gleam and his complexion was pale and waxy. Ralph Kettle leaned in closer to hear him speak.

'Who shot me? *Quien?*' Rico gasped tiredly.

'It was Finch,' John Fishback replied quickly. 'You know it, don't you, Rico?'

'It wasn't him. He had no gun . . . was in front,' Rico growled. 'The shot came from behind. It wasn't Finch,' he said, then his eyelids flickered and closed.

'*Esta muerto?*' one of the two Mexicans asked.

'Not yet. But he's too weak to talk any more,' Ralph Kettle straightened and faced the tall foreman. 'That just about settles it, John. Finch is off your hook.'

Fishback's eyes flicked to Jack.

'No he's not. What the hell do we know about him? How do we know he hasn't got a partner up on the timber line? How do we know they don't aim to rustle all your stock when the time's right? How do we know that Ralph — ?'

'Because I'm not as lackbrained as you, Fishback,' Jack retorted. 'If there is any rustling going on I'd say it starts a lot closer to home.'

Colour rose up from the foreman's neck.

'Damn you, Finch,' he cursed. 'Do you want to back that up with somethin'?'

'Shut up, the both o' you,' Kettle shouted. 'John, get back to the bunkhouse. I want to have a few words with Finch The rest of you clear out. The ranch doesn't run itself.'

The two Mexicans left at once. John Fishback didn't budge, his stance was challenging.

'Considerin', I'd like to hear what it is you're talkin' to Finch about,' he said.

A nerve tugged under Kettle's right eye as he indicated the open study door.

'You're getting way above your station, John. Shut the door on your way out,' he rasped. A moment later, Kettle turned to Jack.

'He's got no class, along with most of us gringos,' he said with a weary smile. 'This is a bad business, Jack. I can understand why him and the others are in a blue funk. Rico's shot in the back and the killer's probably still around somewhere. We don't know what the hell's happening. Do you?'

'Me?' Jack was baffled. 'Why should I?'

'Well, you were with him . . . Rico. Why weren't you shot? Were you even shot at? You never said. I mean, will they want another go? For whatever reason?'

'How the hell do I know? I told you, I didn't see anyone. Maybe he got scared and hightailed. It happens you know, unless you're a natural born killer.'

'And it happens the day after you arrive?'

'Goddamnit. I don't normally believe in coincidences, but right now I can't think it's anything else.'

Jack suddenly felt a clench in his vitals. He broke into a sweat and his skin crawled when it came to him. It was Dawson Cayne. The man had followed him from Whitewater. It was Cayne's bullet that had nearly killed Rico. In the stable, when he'd called for water, it was Cayne who'd been there.

'What is it?' Kettle interrupted Jack's thoughts. 'What're you thinking?'

Jack squeezed his empty glass as if something would emerge. How could he even start to explain his predicament: that a mankiller had followed him to Ralph Kettle's home. What if he was wrong, that it was only some halfwit brand-burner who'd lost the beef he'd stolen from Kettle, and in a panic had shot Rico? Then again, if it was Dawson Cayne, surely he'd be dead, or Rico would have been allowed to kill him. No, it can't be him, Jack was deciding. He couldn't have found me, he thought.

'My head's reeling,' he said. 'Must be the morphine fumes, or whatever that doctor used on Rico. It's taking me back to the sanatorium.'

'Well, sit down, I've got an antidote for that. Besides, there's something I'd like to tell you,' Kettle said.

Jack watched Kettle pour a generous measure of whiskey from a decanter. He felt exhausted, like a flattened bulldog rider. He took the heavy shot glass, tilted it backwards and forwards, considering what effect the whiskey might have. Then he drank it in one gulp.

'Yeah, that's the way to take your finest corn,' Kettle mocked. Sitting opposite Jack, behind his desk, the rancher eyed the golden liquor in his own glass. 'You've obviously had some ideas about John Fishback and Walter Bishop,' he said, avoiding the look that Jack gave him. 'Well, let me say I know about the rustling. I sort of ignore it. It's penny-ante stuff, just a few head now and then for their Friday nights in town. It's a small price to pay. We all get our bread buttered.'

'What's it a small price for?' Jack asked.

'My safeguarding.'

'And what do you need safeguarding from?'

'That's what I want to tell you about,' Kettle started. 'Ten years back I owned a ranch up north of the Plateau, near Flagstaff. It was near the same size as this one. One day my foreman caught one of the hands being too liberal with an iron. I had him arrested and he went to Phoenix to serve time. He swore at his trial he'd kill me when he got out. Hell, it was callow anger, and I was younger and hot-headed.

'However, I took his threat serious, sold out and headed for Mexico with my wife and daughter. I was pretending to act in the interests of their safety. But it was my own skin I was scared for, not

164

theirs. I even changed our name to Kettle. Constanza has never known her real name.'

'Which is?' Jack asked, thinking it might be relevant.

'Don't matter. I'm telling you this because I know that you of all people will understand.'

'Right,' Jack replied, not at all certain that he did. His mind wasn't totally on Kettle's story. He was thinking that Dawson Cayne could be somewhere outside right now, with his rifle, just waiting. He looked at his empty glass, thought that maybe Kettle was reluctant to offer him another good whiskey.

Rico muttered in Spanish in his fevered sleep. Thoughtfully, Kettle considered the man's words, then put down his own glass and continued:

'I'm not a coward, Jack but I'm not a brave man, either. I bought this spread because it was near three hundred miles from Flagstaff . . . seemed safe enough. You'd think my past was dead and buried, but every day of my life I half-expected to see him when I turned around. Every time a stranger rode in I died a little. I hired Bishop and Fishback because they were bad enough to match the son of a bitch. That is something you'll understand, eh Jack?'

★　★　★

Long after he'd left Kettle, as Jack lay in the bunkhouse, he could hear the pathetic tone of Kettle's voice, confessing in the hope that maybe a problem shared would be a problem halved.

'Hah! Closer to telling me, in the hope I'll take care of it,' he muttered into the darkness.

Kettle's wife had died about three years after the family had arrived in Mexico, but Constanza had gone back across the border to find work in Whitewater. Consequently, Kettle got older and more frightened, remaining in hiding from an ironic fear. Why the hell should I understand that? Jack thought.

But he slept fully clothed, the fingers of one hand pinching the lucky acorn, the other beneath the pillow, holding his Colt.

★   ★   ★

Jack wakened from a fitful sleep. The wind had dropped, his railroad stemwinder said 4.30. He dressed quietly, carrying his boots past the row of sleeping men, eased open the door to the rudimentary stoop. The rain had stopped, but the early morning was bitterly cold, extraordinarily quiet. Innumerable stars illumined the muddy yard, horses inside the corral moved and snorted expectantly as he approached the stables.

'Raul?' he called quietly. Kicking gummy mud off his soles, he called again.

A match struck behind him and he whirled, pointing his Colt at the spark of flame.

'Easy, feller,' John Fishback said.

'Lookin' for your crazy Mex friend?'

'If I put a bullet in you right now, Fishback, I'd be saving a lot of people a lot of time and trouble,' Jack snapped back. 'Last night Chama was running from your goddamn lynch rope.'

'We were roostered,' the foreman said quietly. 'Hell man, we were scared . . . nervous enough to bite anythin'. So where do you figure he is?'

'Not far. It was too dark for safe riding.'

'Then he'll probably make for the line shack. It's near to where him an' Walt were brandin' yesterday . . . where I'd head if I wanted cover away from the ranch.'

'He'll ride as soon as he can see,' Jack said.

'Daylight's about thirty minutes off. I can show you where it is.'

'Is this your way of showing regret for something, Fishback?'

'That'll be the day,' the foreman spat. 'There ain't too much I like about you, Finch, but I got it wrong about you backshootin' Rico. Perhaps there's somethin' else. Let's saddle up.'

Stars were fading from the eastern sky as they rode from the yard, picking up a trail between south and west of the ranch. Jack felt uneasy riding with Fishback, but in his own basic way the man had apologized. All the same, Jack rode well to the rear and kept his right hand free.

They rode across the low foothills for several miles before reaching a clearing studded with white oak. Winding their way through, they reached a broad, grass-covered rise where RK longhorns moved leisurely at their graze.

'There,' Fishback said, pointing a gloved hand at the ramshackle structure.

'He wouldn't have walked here,' Jack muttered. 'Where's his horse?'

'Maybe we didn't see it back in the trees.'

Both men became guarded, as if a warning had been mooted. They nudged their horses on to the line shack, dismounting quiet and vigilant. Fishback's hard features just about showed in the interior gloom.

'Not here. He's not here,' he breathed.

Jack could make out an empty bunk, a handful of branding irons in a bucket, some old cigarito butts littering the floor.

'But someone's been here,' Fishback continued. 'There's no chill in these blankets yet, so they're not too far away.'

Jack thought for a moment, then stepped back into the fresher air. He was reaching for his saddlehorn when a rifle shot banged and rolled out across the clearing.

Fishback ran out, cursing; stood staring at Jack while the reverberations headed off across the quiet country. Then he ran for his horse, heeling the mount straight into a gallop towards the trees.

Jack followed, trying to grasp the significance of the single shot.

As they ran their mounts clear of the oaks they saw the horse with its neck lowered. It was nosing the body of Raul Chama, who lay motionless at its feet.

They dismounted, pushed the horse aside, knelt either side of the body. There was no need to feel or look for a pulse, a big-calibre bullet had punched out most of the man's throat.

The sky was getting bluer and, east of the trees and rising timber line, they could see for miles, almost back to the ranch house.

Nothing moved other than an early lark and more RK cattle. Fishback was the first to speak.

'Rustlers,' he grated.

'I don't think so,' Jack said, his voice heavy with apprehension.

'Where'd it come from?' Fishback wondered, staring around him. Jack indicated a point somewhere low on the timber line.

'A long ways off. Up there I shouldn't wonder.'

Fishback pulled his rifle from its

saddle scabbard and fired six rounds into the distance.

'Come on, show somethin',' he yelled. 'It's different when you got a man facin' you — eh, you murderin' scum?'

'I wouldn't bet on it,' Jack shouted at him. 'And you're wasting your breath as well as your bullets. He'll not show himself till he's ready.'

Fishback was already shoving more rounds into the magazine. His eyes narrowed. 'Sounds like you know him,' he yelled.

'It's odds on,' Jack replied. 'Give me a hand with Raul.'

14

When the two riders walked the horses into the yard most of the ranch hands moved out to see whose body was being led in. The Mexicans gathered around, looking, reaching out a hand. When they saw Raul Chama was dead, they made the sign of the cross.

'*Vamonos,*' one of them said. 'There's a curse to this place.'

'*Sí,*' another agreed. 'I want my time made up.'

John Fishback dismounted, his eyes glaring towards Jack. He raised a hand for attention.

'Listen to me,' he started. 'We've had ourselves a little trouble here, but that's it now. I'll bring in some law from Aqua Cajon. It won't be long before — '

'Law from Aqua Cajon?' someone broke in with a throaty spit. 'You joke, *señor*? The *viejo* who carries two squirrel guns because he can't see good enough to point a pistol?'

'Yes,' another voice joined in. 'Why should he care what happens? Do you not comprende, señor? Gringos were never welcome. We were foolish to come here. Now we are leaving.'

Fishback cursed, shook his head in hopelessness.

'All right, I'll see Mr Kettle about your pay,' he said. 'Meanwhile, that isn't a gringo lying across the back o' that mare. He's one o' yours, so take his body to the bunkhouse.' The foreman took a few strides towards the house and stopped. 'Later, those who want to move on, come to the house. You too, Finch,' he added.

The men carried Raul Chama to the bunkhouse, laid him on the bunk nearest the door. The man's eyes were still open and Jack leaned in to close the lids.

'Doesn't look like it takes that much to die, does it?' one of the punchers said. 'Why do you do that?'

174

'What?' Jack asked.

'Close his eyes.'

'It's a custom, I guess. I think it's to stop them seeing if they're headed for a bad place.'

Gloomily the other punchers spoke among themselves as they packed their traps. Jack sat on his bunk, looking at Raul Chama. When the men walked into the yard, he followed on.

'Are you leaving?' he asked Hector Bream as he passed the cookhouse.

Bream shrugged, watching as they approached the house where Ralph Kettle, Fishback and Walter Bishop waited on the veranda steps.

'Whoever stays'll need some sort o' grease belly,' he muttered to himself.

'I'm not a man to plead,' Ralph Kettle said when they were gathered in front of the house. 'I can start over, same as before. I know two of you've been shot, and one's dead. But it's the work of one man, and John tells me he's still somewhere in those hills. You hear me? You're all fear-struck over a lone backshooter.'

Jack caught his eye. 'Maybe it's about time I said something . . . told what I know,' he said.

The rancher didn't seem to need the interruption.

'I think I know what you're wanting to say Jack, and it don't make a scrap of difference. Who wants to talk about why a scorpion stings? It just does. The only way to deal with them and other poisonous vermin is to stamp on 'em hard.'

'Maybe. But it's me who's meant to take the sting,' Jack said.

'Not any longer. If any of you men run out today you'll run again tomorrow and the next day. I know because I did it once, hoping hundreds of miles would make me safe. But that's a sort of death too. A living death.'

'It's the dying death that worries us,' another of the Mexicans said. 'Sorry, Señor Kettle, we are going.'

'OK. Pay them off, John,' Kettle told his foreman after a moment of thought.

The men pushed up and Fishback paid them from a wad of banknotes.

'It's not fightin' wages,' he said almost scornfully.

Jack studied the foreman's face. It hadn't occurred to him before that Fishback and Bishop might have motives other than loyalty for not heading south with the Mexicans. Of a sudden, he saw the pair for the opportunists and bottom-dealers they really were.

Ralph Kettle had money in the house. With every one else gone, Fishback and Bishop could do what they wanted. They might even wait until Connie arrived and include her in their family plunder.

'Here's yours, Finch,' Fishback said, counting out a few bills. 'Ain't much but, like I said . . . an' you've only been here three days.'

'I'm not going anywhere.' Jack watched the foreman's features suddenly darken. 'I'm staying with Mr Kettle — if he'll have me, of course,' he replied.

'I wouldn't have expected less,' the rancher said. 'If you'd been with me in Arizona perhaps I wouldn't be here now. Well, we're none of us alone in this. There's me, John, Walt and Hec.'

'Yeah, that's right,' Hector Bream called out. Striding across the yard, the cook pushed through the discomfited Mexicans, thumped a big fist on the hitching pole. 'If it's any o' you that rifleman wants, he'll get you. You ain't goin' to get away from him. As for me, I'm too old an' out o' shape to run anywhere. Besides, I've kind o' got to like livin' here.'

Kettle nodded. 'And I kind o' got used to having you around, Hec. That's the five of us. This hombre who's set on stiffing you, Jack. What can you tell us about him?'

'Not much,' Jack started, having asked himself the same questions many times. 'I don't even know why he wants to kill me. I know why I want to kill him, though. But right now that don't seem like an advantage. I think they call people like him devil-ridden.'

*   *   *

The sun was starting to be overcome by cloud as the Mexicans rode out. Ralph Kettle stood in the middle of the home yard, gazing at the distant Sierras above the heavily wooded foothills.

'Curious, ain't it?' he said to Jack. 'That's what I thought of the feller who chased me across the goddamn Plateau. Sometimes I'd wonder if it was the old boogerman himself.'

'Well, just in case you're wondering, they're not one and the same,' Jack said.

A strange smile turned the rancher's mouth.

'Not the same, but not unalike either. Do you reckon he's up in the hills?'

'Yes, and I think he'll come back down again after dark. He obviously wants to stretch this thing out a bit. He could have killed me last night.'

'Do you know why he didn't?'

'No,' Jack said. 'It's like he's playing out some evil game.'

'Should we hunt him or wait?'

'Wait. That way we have the advantage of surprise. I'd say he's watching, maybe using a glass atop that big cannon. He'll have seen the Mexes ride off.'

'So what do you propose?'

'I'll move off . . . wave my arm as if I'm not taking what you're offering,' Jack explained. 'Fishback and Bishop take a threatening step towards me, then stop. I'll carry on to the stables. It'll look as though we've had an argument . . . that I'm walkin' from a fight. It might draw him in.'

15

The weird, unsettling time of day, in Jack's view, was the hour about first dark. The day was gone and night hadn't yet started. The country looked flat, with little colour or definition. In the stables he sat on a flour barrel, on the same spot he'd been tied the previous night. The ranch looked and sounded like a graveyard. He very slowly rolled the chamber of his Colt with his thumb, wondered if he'd got enough ordnance.

Hector Bream had made him a batch of corn dodgers earlier. They were on a plate near his feet, next to a bottle of Kettle's good whiskey. John Fishback and Walter Bishop had reluctantly agreed to the plan to lure the dry-gulcher down to the ranch. Bishop was positioned inside one of the small outhouses behind the livery stable. His job was to guard any approach from the rear.

Fishback occupied the bunkhouse, waiting for full dark before taking a position near the corral.

Got to be some boogerman to get past that lot, Jack thought, especially if whoever it was also saw Hector Bream sitting under the cookhouse roof with a shotgun across his knees.

The house lights were burning early, but the blinds were drawn. Behind one of the windows Rico tossed and turned in a restless sleep. He was unaware of the hour; at times his ailing growls could be heard across the deep stillness of the yard.

Ralph Kettle sat in a chair on the front veranda. He had two guns, an old army Colt and a fine, over-and-under shotgun. When the strain got too much he walked to the corner of the building, looked towards the distant mountains.

They'd expect to see the ranch taking steps to protect itself, Jack considered. None of those left would want to be murdered in their sleep.

It was full dark when Jack heard the horses snorting and nickering, telling him Fishback was taking his position near the corral. Quiet returned after a few seconds. All it needed was for Dawson Cayne to arrive.

Jack took another mouthful of whiskey. In his mind's eye he saw his father's weather-worn face, as it had been during his boyhood in San Simon. A time of games, hunting and fishing, hanging around the ranch where his pa worked. Funning with Will Morgan and little Bean Decker, watching their fathers' exploits, rounding up cattle.

Jack suddenly frowned at his own thoughtful memories. There was a morose straw-haired kid who hung back, watching, never joining in. That was Dawson Cayne as a child. The bright, good-natured boy all the kids admired was his brother, Lew. It had been a bad day indeed when the balky claybank had thrown him.

Jack heard a sound and sat up, eased

the hammer of his Colt back slowly. His childhood memories disappeared fast as he confronted the darkness.

'Ease off the trigger, Jack,' a voice called in a whisper. 'It's me, Kettle.'

'Pheew, you should have stayed where you were,' Jack said. 'I could've shot you for being him.'

'Yeah, but I guessed you'd want to see the whites of his eyes before pulling the trigger. I thought I'd seen someone over this way and came to find out . . . to give you this.'

Kettle stepped forward and handed Jack a Henry repeater.

'Finest rifle in these parts,' he said. 'I've no real need for it; thought you might put it to use. I've noticed the piece you've been hanging on to.'

'Thanks, Mr Kettle, that's real thoughtful,' Jack said. 'But hell, you were taking a chance. It was probably Fishback you saw. You best let him know you're here. And act normal. We don't want our guest to know we're ready and waiting for him.'

Jack heard an exchange of words between Kettle and his foreman. He meant well, Jack thought. Could have spooked Cayne, though.

He holstered his Colt, picked up and chewed on a corn dodger, was contemplating another when a big-bore rifle barrel jabbed him hard below his ear.

'I'm back. Don't choke yourself just yet,' the voice of Dawson Cayne rasped.

Jack felt the man's hand lift his Colt.

'Playing games again?' he said. 'If you're not going to shoot me, Cayne, what the hell sort of game are you playing?'

'It's not much of a game that's soonest over,' the man replied. 'No, this is somethin' that needs time. When we were in Cerro Cubacho you asked me why. Well, killin' you without you knowin' it, ain't an agreeable vengeance, is it?'

'There's only one person who vengeance belongs to, and you ain't him, you crazy son of a bitch.'

'It's for the death of my brother Lew, and my pa.'

'I just said you were crazy, Cayne. I didn't know it, just guessed. Now I know.'

'You know nothin', Jack boy. Hell, why do you think I didn't kill you when you were huntin' them lost cattle? I had you cold in my sights . . . could've lain you to rest real easy. But it wouldn't have served. I shot your big Mex friend to let you know I was around.'

'He wasn't a friend, Cayne. But Chama was. Or as near to one as damnit.'

'Oh yeah. I knew that.'

Feeling as if cold, bony fingers were clutching at his vitals, Jack was beginning to better understand the malice of Dawson Cayne.

'You killed Raul Chama because he was my friend?' he rasped.

'Sure I did, and I've an eye for that pretty Whitewater nurse. But that's for after I've settled you. Somehow I'm makin' up for what your pa and the others did.'

186

'You're talking gibberish, Cayne. What the hell's my pa got to do with this?'

'Don't you remember the day my brother died?'

'Yeah, I remember. He was thrown from a horse.'

'Did you know, your pa and them other two were wagering on my brother? Lew didn't want to ride. He thought he'd be considered yellow if he backed down. So he climbed on that claybank beast and got himself killed, and others made money from it.'

Sweat covered Jack's face, ran between his shoulder blades.

'So, and after all this time you decided to shoot a few people . . . innocent people.'

'I never set out to shoot anyone. My pa made me promise when he left us. It was him tried to shoot your pa an' the others when he learned how Lew died. They arrested him for attemptin' it, but he was already goin' mad. He got worse after that an' they shifted him to a nuthouse in the middle of a goddamn forest. Every other month, me an' Ma went to visit him.'

Jack listened quietly. He realized the man was close to an overwhelming, emotional crisis, that if he, Jack, made a wrong move, Cayne would probably shoot him. 'What about her . . . your ma? What did she want?' he asked flatly.

'I don't know. She never said. I got home one day and she was sitting in her chair staring out the widow with a half-smile on her face. She died that way . . . just given up.'

The ensuing silence was bad. It was a few more moments before Cayne continued.

'I had a dead ma and a crazy pa. That ain't much for a youngster. Pa didn't last long after that. He made me promise to do the killings. 'Vengeance is mine', he said. But I think he meant me.' Cayne went quiet for a while. 'There was no money to give either of 'em a decent-lookin' plot,' he said.

'That's too bad, Cayne. And you

were both wrong. You and your pa. So what now . . . now the talking's done? Maybe you won't hang on grounds of derangement, indisputable motive or something. If not, you'll have to kill again. If I live, somehow I'll kill you. That's called self-defence, and it's legal.'

Cayne backed off.

'I promised Pa,' he said after a long pause. 'That's more or less what I came to tell you. Meantime, you're goin' to breathe shallow, wonderin' when.'

Jack was already considering his escape, crouching to be nearer the hard-packed dirt floor. He sprang up, leapt forward bending low, took six fast and desperate steps out through the double doors into the night.

He hadn't got to the safety cover of anywhere before a bright flame ignited ahead of him. He threw himself down as the rifle blasted off in front and to the side. He knew it was difficult for Cayne to make a shot from behind him. He wouldn't have time to aim, and it was dark. But he'd overlooked Fishback, who was ready and waiting for the opportunity. He cursed as the foreman's bullet snatched at the ground beside him. He stared up ahead, in the flash of light saw the man's face, the glistening, gimlet eyes, the gun barrel levelling for a more measured shot.

The rifle shot crashed out madly, the orange flame lighting the yawning darkness of the livery entrance. Ahead of him John Fishback dropped his rifle, took a step back and collapsed, falling face down and dead into the yard.

Ralph Kettle ran from the house. He was joined by Walter Bishop even before he reached Fishback's body.

'What the hell happened?' he shouted.

Jack, blinking himself into alertness, staggered to his feet.

'I don't know,' he told them. 'But it's Cayne, like I said. He was in the barn. I ran out and Fishback fired. It must have been Cayne who shot him.'

Kettle and Bishop peered around

them into the darkness, back towards the livery.

'Is he still in there?' Kettle asked.

'I guess so,' Jack said. 'He's not got many options left.'

Hector Bream called out from the cookhouse. 'That's where the shot came from, an' no one's come out. Is Fishback hurt bad?'

'He's dead,' Bishop yelled back.

'You want me out there with you?'

'No, Hec. Get yourself around the barn — behind it,' Kettle replied. 'Shout out when you're there. We've got the front covered.'

Kettle handed Jack the big Army Colt. 'You're sure working your way through my gun rack, son,' he said. 'Let's hope you soon get to use one.'

'John's dead,' Bishop said bleakly. 'What is happenin' here?'

'There's something I don't understand,' the rancher said, turning to Jack. 'If John was shooting at you, why should he care? You reckon he's still in the barn?'

191

'Yeah, quietly waiting to make his escape, I shouldn't wonder,' Jack said.

'You didn't answer me,' Kettle pursued. 'Why should he care who shoots you?'

'Because he wants to do it . . . in time. It's his killing game. And this isn't the time or place to explain.'

'Me an' John should have gone with the Mexicans. All of us should,' Bishop muttered.

'I can't see anythin',' Hector Bream suddenly called out. 'It's as black as pitch.'

'So let's go,' Kettle said, and with all guns actioned, the three men advanced warily on the barn.

'I've got a lamp. I'll light it when we get up close,' Bishop breathed. 'I'll toss it inside. If he's in there we'll know soon enough.'

'The man I've just met probably likes flames around him,' Jack replied caustically.

At the entrance Walter Bishop struck a match and lit the lantern. The moment the light grew he looked at Kettle, who nodded. He hurled the lamp inside, it flew in a big arc that took it a long way into the barn.

The flames grew instantly and Jack saw that Cayne was at the rear of the building, where a crude ladder led to the hay loft.

'No way out up there, Señor Diablo,' he mumbled. 'That's your first mistake.'

Bishop ran into the barn, in one movement scooped up the lamp and overarmed it up to the hayloft. The atmosphere, thick with dust and dry duff practically exploded. Instantly a burst of flame billowed and filled the vaulted roof space.

Clambering on to the platform of beams, Cayne became lost in the roiling blaze.

'The whole barn's going to burn,' Kettle yelled. 'There's nothing we can do now. Back off.'

'There's a couple o' horses in there,' Bishop gasped.

A section of clapboard wall was now

running with flames rising from the floor.

Kettle took a long, tortured look and shook his head.

'I know. I know. But it's too late.'

Jack looked up, thought he saw Cayne trying to beat away the engulfing flames. Some of the roof shingles fell away. They landed as sparkling embers on the loft's puncheon beams, and rafters lit up one by one as the fire took hold.

16

Hector Bream's eyes were large in the firelight. He held up a hand to shield his face against the heat from the disintegrating building.

'Nothing can stop it,' Ralph Kettle muttered, staring in shock and disbelief. 'We're lucky there's no wind tonight.'

Jack looked around for Bishop, saw him kneeling beside Fishback's body.

'He's dead. What are you looking for?' he asked.

Bishop rose to his feet. 'He owed me twenty dollars. I got ten of 'em. I can't afford not to.'

'Fair enough,' Jack replied.

Kettle pointed for Bream to let the panicky horses out of the corral.

'Don't worry,' he called. 'They'll run 'emselves out and come home, eventually.'

'How many did we lose?' the cook asked.

'I don't think we lost any in the end. The shavetails kicked their way out and ran off towards the lower pasture. They'll come back too, when they realize there's only grass and water down there.'

'You think he's still in here?' Bishop asked.

'He didn't look like he was going far the last time I saw him,' Jack said. 'But nothing's certain.'

The barn was a mass of low flames, cinders and pungent smoke. The whole building had been gutted in a matter of minutes, there had never been any chance of putting the fire out. Watching the falling embers, Kettle told Bishop and Bream to fill water buckets and carry them to the main house.

'In case the wind gets up,' he explained. He turned to Jack. 'I asked you why Cayne should stop John from shooting you. You didn't say.'

'I did. I told you. He wants to be the one to do it.'

'So why didn't he?'

'If he'd known he was going to die there and then, he would have,' Jack replied. Kettle looked back at the fire.

'Then you figure he's dead?'

'If he's in here, yes. He came down with the loft beams and the rafters on top of him. Who could live through that?'

'Tomorrow we'll check the place out. There's plenty more whiskey in the house if you want, Jack.'

'No thanks. I'll stay here till the fire burns itself out.'

'Can't think what the hell for. I'm going back. Join me if you change your mind.'

Jack didn't reply as Kettle walked off towards the house. He felt the lucky acorn given him by Connie and gave a thin smile. She was due to arrive early the following week, but now the two men who were a risk to her safety were dead. He'd reckoned on staying about ten days, so he wasn't too far out. Besides, he wanted to know about his bayo mare, and he ought to tell her the *bona fortuna* acorn was still working.

Rubbing circulation and feeling back into his arms and legs, Jack looked at the body of John Fishback. Maybe he should have got help to carry him inside, but he didn't.

'I'm not that big a fraud,' he muttered, guessing that Kettle had felt the same.

★   ★   ★

The lamp was out when Bream and Bishop entered the bunkhouse and laid Fishback's body out on a bunk.

'At least he ain't a mean son of a bitch any longer,' Bishop said. He darted a glance towards Jack. 'You awake there?'

Jack didn't move or say anything. He wasn't faking sleep, just lying tired and silent.

'I guess we can all rest a little easier now that backshootin' snake's got burned,' Bream said.

'Hey, Jack,' Bishop continued, 'Tomorrow we'll go look for that devil man o' yours. Perhaps we can make medicine bones from him, like the Apaches do with us white folk.'

'Shut it, Walt,' Bream snapped. 'You're just jealous 'cause he's sleepin'. It's sure what I'd like to be.'

Bream and Bishop were snoring long before Jack found his own sleep. In his mind he'd shot Dawson Cayne dead a dozen times and in as many ways. But in the real, he'd never got the chance to fire a single shot at his wife's killer. What troubled him was whether he would have been able to face Cayne in a cold shoot-out. He was no gunsman, so would his hand and heart remain steady? Would he ever know for sure?

His eyes were open when daylight coloured the bunkhouse windows. He was eager, uncaring and reluctant all at the same time, to see how real the night's events had been. Not having bothered to undress in the early hours, he was soon up and stepping out into the cold morning.

Jack pulled the door to behind him and stared at the fire-rased building across the yard. Only the main structure remained, blackened posts that fingered the pale sky. He used a hay fork to poke and turn the charred debris. Ten minutes later Walter Bishop was standing beside him.

'You ain't found anythin', have you?' the man almost whispered.

'No, but he's here someplace. I saw him on fire. Help me look.'

'Where? We'd have to dig to Hades to find him, an' you know it.'

Jack felt a splash of rain on the back of his hand and lifted his eyes to the early light. He swore and speared the fork into the ashes.

'He's still alive,' Bishop said. 'You best pack an' run, Jack, 'cause it ain't us he's after.'

Jack knuckled his eyes. 'He's flesh and blood like you and me. So wherever he is, whatever the hell he's doing, he's burnt bad.' He brushed past the burly man and looked around the yard, out towards the hills.

'Figurin' on riding after him?'

'Something like that,' Jack grunted. 'Is there a spare saddle?'

'There's stuff in the tack house. Want me to go find a horse?'

'No, I think I'll do this on my own. Thanks.'

'Do what on your own?' a voice said.

Jack turned to face Ralph Kettle.

'Nothing here but the barn, eh Jack?' the rancher said gravely. 'Hell, I can see it in your face. Walt, wake up Hec. Get some rope and fetch us some horses. I've got to go see a man about something.'

'Hold on a minute. This is my trouble,' Jack protested.

'That's more or less what you said yesterday, son,' Kettle said and nodded at Bishop. 'Get the horses.' Then he turned back to Jack. 'Don't you understand?' Kettle appealed. 'This is my chance to face up to something.'

'I understand that, but this isn't to do

with you,' Jack said firmly. 'It wasn't your wife.'

'But this is my ranch, and they're my men he's killed. That's worth a ride with you, surely?'

'Look, Mr Kettle, do you think I'm looking forward to pitting myself against a malicious psychopath? You think I'll hold out if and when I find him?'

'I don't rightly know. You're not running away like I did.'

Jack nodded. 'That's because for me, running to and running from've become the same thing. My guts were in real trouble last night when Cayne held a gun to my head. That's not happening again.'

'Let me help. I really do understand.'

'OK. Maybe you're owed that. As long as you also understand that if Cayne's still alive not all of us will be coming back.'

17

An hour before noon the four men began their climb. It was at the place from where Rico had been shot. Stopping, they peered upward.

'From here on in you could be in his sights,' Jack said. 'One thing's for sure, he was hurt by fire and in pain. But don't rely upon it slowing him down.'

Amid the trees he picked up a cartridge case and showed it to the others.

'This is about where he fired on Rico,' he said, turning over the brass case. 'Probably a .50-calibre buffalo rifle.'

'I used to own a fine Henry repeater,' Kettle said, without nuance or even a glance towards Jack. 'But I've brought a Sharps big fifty along. Didn't think I'd ever use either of 'em.'

Jack eyed the big rifle protruding

from the rancher's saddle scabbard.

'Let's continue hoping you don't,' he said. 'From here on we go slow and separate. Keep looking ahead, try not to give him target. But if he opens up, try to go to ground, fast.'

The riders were fatigued with nervous tension when they cleared the trees and confronted the foothills.

'Let's haul in for a moment,' Bishop gasped. 'I haven't breathed for ten minutes.'

Kettle eased himself from the saddle, sat quietly on a low rocky mound.

Jack took a searching look around him, his eyes following a course that wound up towards a towering, craggy outcrop. He looked for a shape, a movement, anything that might give Cayne's position away.

'You're up there somewhere, you son of a bitch,' he muttered as he dismounted. Hector Bream sat beside him.

'What happens after we get this Cayne feller?' he asked. 'You sure won't be settlin' down here.'

'I haven't thought that far ahead. How about you, Hec? Are you staying on at the RK?'

The man gave a wily grin. 'I would like to go home, but I ain't got one. I've been workin' between here an' the Colorado since I was knee high. So, when all this is done, what say you an' me go partners? We can ride to one o' them land states an' get a passel? A hundred an' twenty acres, I hear.'

'It's a thought. Why not?' Jack said. It was why not because Jack hadn't considered doing anything beyond Dawson Cayne. Of a sudden, the ranch's biscuit roller was talking about life the day after.

'Come on,' Kettle said. 'The day's not getting any longer.' The rancher grabbed his horse, checking that his rifle was secure.

Bishop frowned at the mountains above and beyond.

'Given a chance, I'm goin' to do somethin' real bad when we meet that polecat,' he asserted. 'John Fishback was one of us.'

They climbed higher until the air thinned and they were once again exhausted. The snow line was getting closer, and they could feel its chill, blowing across their faces. Jack looked at his stemwinder and shook his head.

'We'll have to head back now if we want to beat the dark. Else we camp here for the night.'

'We make camp. I'm not turning back,' Kettle said stubbornly. 'A fire might draw him in.'

'Goddamnit again,' Bream complained, sitting down and starting to remove a boot. 'I didn't reckon on bein' your mantrap.'

'You're not,' Kettle replied. 'Unless you're close up to the fire he won't know where the hell you are. That goes for all of us. The man's going to be colder'n a witch's tit tonight. He'll either want his own fire or ours. Either way, he loses. You understand me?'

Bishop's eyes creased up with thinking.

'Sounds like you been at the jimson, boss,' he said. 'Now you got sand for us all.'

The words hit Kettle like a punch in the belly. He shook his head, stared thoughtfully into the middle distance.

Bishop pulled a bottle from his hip pocket, bit out the cork and held it out to Kettle.

'Here, boss,' he said with a near smirk. 'It ain't your usual tipple. But it'll help you with your daring.'

Jack didn't move. His expression hardly changed as he watched Kettle reach out for whatever crude spirit Bishop was offering.

★   ★   ★

After a late meal of coffee-soaked corn dodgers Kettle, Bream and Bishop were slowly falling into a thin, fitful sleep. But Jack wasn't. He waited until deep into the night, then rolled free of his blanket, grabbed his Winchester with the wrecked stock and slipped quietly away from the camp.

Skirting the edge of the tree line, he took up a position beside an ancient blowdown pine, less than fifty yards from the sleeping men. He turned his collar, blew on the backs of his hands and lifted the rifle to his shoulder. Above the still-distant peaks stars glistened in the thin, chill air. The available light afforded a good view up and down the mountainside.

After an hour of intense concentration his eyes were beginning to ache and break up his vision. He heard a slight sound and looked towards the sleeping camp. Something that wasn't a night critter was moving stealthily through the trees, coming his way.

Nestling the rifle stock against his shoulder, he blinked, squinted down the sights. Should be OK with this, he thought of his Winchester. At this distance the buffalo gun would take out half the surrounding timber.

Walter Bishop broke from the darkness and Jack's trigger finger relaxed. He exhaled a relieved breath and called out, irritated.

'Get back to the camp.'

'He's gone,' Bishop replied. 'I've come to find you.'

Jack cursed and leapt to his feet; then, Jack indicating that Bishop should go ahead, they quickly made their way back to camp.

'He just upped and left, did he?' Jack asked, seeing the empty bedroll.

'No. The horses were restless, an' he went to check 'em. That was about half an hour ago.'

He won't be coming back was Jack's first thought. He felt it in his gut. He glanced at Kettle, but the old man was still sleeping soundly. Bishop stared at Jack as though he, Jack, had the answer.

'What d'you reckon?' he said.

'We'll go and see,' Jack replied. 'Lead the way, I'll cover you.'

A minute or so later, Bishop cursed breathlessly.

'They're gone. Our goddamn mounts are gone.'

'Of course they are,' Jack snapped, then listened intently. The vague figure caught Jack's eye as it rose and stumbled forward, towards them.

'Hey, who the hell slugged me?' Hector Bream slurred.

'His name's Dawson Cayne, and you're lucky he didn't slit your throat,' Jack said.

The three men stood silent. They could hear the horses moving back down the slope, the sound of someone groaning in pain.

'What the hell do we do now?' Bishop whispered.

'You should've thought of that before riding up here,' Jack muttered.

'I wasn't goin' to be left on my own,' Bishop rejoined gloomily.

'Just stay here.' Jack ran towards the trees below them, alert for any other other sound.

'Jack . . . Jack Finch.' The plaintive cry came again out of the darkness ahead of him. With his blood running cold, Jack tried to figure out the situation. The voice was Ralph Kettle's. But he was rolled in his blanket, sleeping his way to morning.

Kettle's voice came again. 'Jack, are you out there?' Jack cursed, turned back and shouted ahead:

'Hunker down. Cayne's at the camp.'

Immediately, the thunderous blast of a big rifle shook the air and the bulky figure of Walter Bishop came barging through the timber. The man went into a headlong plunge, hit the ground and rolled into a stilled, untidy heap.

'You all right, Hec?' Jack called out, while the echo of the gun's blast reverberated around them.

'Yeah, I'm OK. Walt's down.'

'I know, I saw. You stay put, I'll come to you,' Jack shouted. He ran quickly through the trees, climbing at an angle to the gradient.

Breaking out into the starry night, and a distance from the camp, Jack rushed on to a clump of moss-covered boulders. He hunkered behind them, his finger lightly tapping the curve of the rifle's trigger. Cayne was unpredictable but he had guts. He'd got among them, lain in a bedroll right under their noses and taken Bishop with a single shot, albeit with a bullet big enough to down a full-grown oak.

Jack doubted Cayne was still in the camp. More likely he was going higher above the tree line. He'd be a bit more confident now, probably watch and wait on his next chance. And what of Ralph Kettle? After a few minutes of quiet Jack made a circuitous approach to the camp. He kicked the empty bedroll, called out for Hector Bream. The RK cook staggered forward.

'How the hell did the goddamn fiend manage this?' he gasped. Jack was unsure how to answer.

'Let's see what's happened to Kettle,' he said.

'What about Walt?'

'There's no saving him, Hec. He was dead before he fell.'

How many more would die before it was over, Jack wondered. It sounded as though it was all because, many years in the past, a youngster broke his neck after being thrown from a mustang. But what was it that made Lew Cayne's death so different? What was it really all about?

18

The old man had a bad headache and the side of his face was bruised and swollen. He sat huddled in blankets shaking non-stop, making demands for whiskey.

'There's no drink o' that sort left,' Bream told him. 'When we get back to the ranch there'll be all you want.'

'But not before tomorrow,' Jack furthered.

They'd talked about their situation, decided that at first light they'd slip down the mountainside and head back to the ranch. In a suitable place, Jack would lie in wait for Dawson Cayne while the others went on ahead.

Bream and Jack took turns keeping watch. There wasn't any sleep. It was a break for their strained minds and bodies, although Ralph Kettle noisily complained throughout the dark hours.

'There'll be light in another half-hour,' Jack said. 'I'm going down to find the horses . . . see if there's any rotgut in Bishop's saddle-bags. We need something as much as the old man.'

'Amen. You do that,' Bream said.

The horses were together, standing in a clearing about fifty yards away. Jack moved calmly forwards, quartering the land around them, keeping his rifle lowered.

Poking around in the saddle-bags of Bishop's mare, he found a half-bottle of mescal. He took a long pull, coughed, spat, wiped the back of his hand across his mouth and cursed.

Ten minutes later Kettle's eyes lit up in the early light as he sucked at the fiery liquid. His body shivers eased to a hand tremble, but his voice was full of distress.

'Where is he?' he asked. 'Where is the devil killer?'

'Not far away,' Jack said. 'What did happen here?'

'He's a goddamn banshee . . . like

something you read about,' the rancher muttered. 'I remember Hec going to check on the horses. When he didn't come back, Walt went looking for you. That's when he jumped me. I wasn't fully out but I couldn't get to my feet. When I did, I hit my head on a tree. I think I went down again. Don't remember too much clearly after that. Not until . . . '

'You were shouting my name,' Jack said.

'Yeah, I remember that. And Walt's gone?'

Jack nodded. Kettle took another gulp of the liquor.

'We'd best get on,' he said; Jack wondered whether in the past the man had had some problem with alcohol.

'We're going back to the ranch,' he said. 'And go easy on that stuff.'

'You want us to skedaddle?'

'Yeah, back to home ground. Where you should have stayed. All three of you.'

'Running away again . . . scared

216

spitless,' Kettle said bitterly.

Well, you'd know, was Jack's immediate thought. They were soon ready to move out, Bream helping Kettle and Jack hastily packing the bedrolls and gear. As he was bringing the horses in, he saw the shaken look in Bream's face.

'What's happened now?' he demanded.

'It's Walt,' Bream said. 'He's not there.'

'Well, he wasn't in any fit state to start out on his own,' Jack responded, a little snappier than he meant. 'You looked in the right place?'

'Yeah. He's just not there,' the man replied flatly.

★ ★ ★

They searched all the way to the bottom of the timbered slope, while the old man huddled among the horses.

'Like I said,' the cook huffed. 'It ain't so much this turkey, Cayne, but somethin' else. I think I'll keep ridin', with or without you.'

'After,' Jack grated. 'Our only chance of beating him is to stay together. Even more so now.'

The pair went back up the slope and helped Kettle on to his horse.

'You won't be much use with this,' Jack said, taking the big Sharps rifle.

Bream got mounted, took the reins of Kettle's horse, and moved off.

Jack watched them go, then walked his mount down through the trees. He didn't look up, he just sensed the malevolent eyes watching from above.

As he moved out of the barrier of trees he knew that not even Cayne's buffalo gun could reach him at that range. Or it could, but the chances of making a fatal hit were minimal.

Up ahead, Kettle and Bream dipped over the far side of an arroyo. Jack caught up, reined in and dismounted in the bed of the dried-out creek. If anyone wanted to see where the riders had disappeared to, he just might make himself visible at that point. Jack pulled the Sharps from his saddle roll, leaned against the low, steep walls and peered at the mountains behind him. He blinked against the morning brightness; thought there might be a chance of seeing Cayne emerge from the trees at the base of the timber line.

He saw a condor circling lazily above the pine.

'We travel the same roads,' he muttered, wondering if the big vulture had something in its sights. He twisted around; in the other direction he saw Kettle and Bream being swallowed up by the heat haze and undulating ground. It would be another hour before they reached the ranch, the shelter of timbered walls and a bunk, and plenty of ammunition.

The rancher and Bream dropped from direct sight again. Jack fought away edginess, only to be overcome by a huge fatigue. For two nights he'd had virtually no sleep; now, with the sun on his back, he closed his eyes, considered giving in and riding away. But it was a weak moment and short-lived.

A single horseman was riding from the trees.

Jack laid the Sharps across the top edge of the arroyo. He lined up the sights just before the rider vanished into a sandy dip. He counted the seconds before the rider reappeared, telling himself not to squeeze the trigger too early.

Come close. Come real close and I'll blow your pieces to Yuma, he thought as the distance between them closed. As he let go of his breath his finger slightly increased its pressure on the trigger.

The horse's rhythmic footfalls grew louder as the rider approached. Jack tried to dissolve into the sandy ridge, wondering why the rider was making himself a sitting duck.

The rider was now outlined against the sky. Instead of pulling the trigger Jack hesitated, rolled sideways, sliding back to the dry floor of the arroyo. A nerve-racking uncertainty suddenly ran through his mind.

Why? What's he trying to do?

Jack was avoiding being kicked or trampled, but the horse and rider turned sideways on to him, then pulled away, along the edge of the narrow gully. The hoofs missed him by a few inches, the horse twisting away as it saw him almost beneath its feet.

'That's why,' Jack gasped as he realized. 'It's Walter Bishop. An' he's deader'n hell.' Bishop's large body had been unrecognizable, his features blurred in the shimmer of heat.

Jack switched his attention back towards the mountains. But there was nothing to see and he stared after the corpse on the galloping horse.

What the hell sort of game's that? he wondered. Or are you trying to draw my position — my fire, you son of a bitch?'

He rammed the Sharps back into his bedroll and mounted his horse, bending low and forward in the saddle. A massive rain cloud obscured the still rising sun. The landscape darkened and Jack didn't feel quite so warm any more. What would Cayne do now? he wondered. Maybe move along the lower tree line. Maybe ride in to the ranch from further north. Maybe from where he was right now. Jack hadn't yet shown himself, so Cayne had no idea that he was in the arroyo and hidden from view. If his plan was to follow them, Jack for once had the advantage.

19

The rain had started to fall from a slate-coloured sky as Jack reached the ranch. The stark isolation of the buildings, the barren, muddy yard with its burnt-out barn gave an air of hushed menace. There were three horses tied to the hitching rail in front of the house.

He dismounted, unpacked his bed-roll; a moment later the front door opened. Hector Bream stepped out, relaxing immediately, his shoulders sagging with relief as he saw Jack. Jack climbed the steps and followed him inside.

'Dawson Cayne won't come stepping up to the front door, but lock it anyway,' he warned. The confidence faded from Bream's face.

'Did you miss him?'

'No, I never saw him,' Jack said,

turning to see Ralph Kettle appear from the study.

'You were laying for him. What happened?' Kettle asked.

'I ran into Walt Bishop,' Jack said, and started his explanation. He saw their expressions change from apprehension to near terror.

'I did warn you. The man's becoming a fantasy . . . using a goddamn cadaver to get what he wants. I reckon he'll ride the top pastures and hit us here sometime tonight. There's nothing unreal about that.'

'Why tonight? Why the hell us?' Bream wanted to know.

'Because his enemy's friends become his enemies too. The game he's playing can't be entertaining any more . . . not even for him. He's probably ready for a kill.'

Jack looked inside the study where the Mexican was lying on an improvised cot. Rico forced a weak smile, lifted an arm in recognition.

'No hard feelings, *amigo*,' he said.

Not fully understanding what Rico meant, Jack smiled and shook his head. Kettle's house help, Ramon, sat in a high-backed chair loading an old trade musket. He looked up and nodded.

'Is there anyone else here in the house?' Jack asked.

'No. It's just us,' Kettle said.

'*Cinco contra uno*,' Rico croaked from the cot. 'You think we should worry?'

'Yeah, some. You'll only be of help if he's here in the room. If that happens, it's probably *buenos noches* time. I suggest we get some rest before dark. Maybe Ramon can keep watch while we all close our eyes.'

The men positioned themselves about the room, deliberately not in a direct line of any attack through a window.

After what seemed like minutes to Jack, a hand touched his shoulder. He looked up and saw that Ramon had stacked the fireplace with heavy kindling and set it alight using duff from a tinder box. Hector Bream was holding out a mug of coffee.

'Six o'clock,' he said. 'Took it upon myself to give you a shake. Estimatin' chuck time's what I'm good at.'

Jack sat up and took a sip. 'Thanks Hec. I didn't think hot coffee could be so welcome.'

Ralph Kettle was standing by the window.

'Rain's going to bring on the dark. We'd best eat early,' he said.

Ramon agreed, said that he'd fix something up. He walked from the study with his unwieldy gun and Jack followed him to the kitchen and scullery. One large window revealed rain slanting across colourless foothills and blurry mountains.

'The country's not always beautiful,' Jack said thoughtfully.

'Certainly not a good time for seeing much, señor,' Ramon replied.

'No, but he's out there, Ramon. I can feel him.' For a moment, Jack watched Ramon attend to the stove. 'What other windows or doors are back here?' he asked.

'*Una momento*,' Ramon said. He shoved a heavy frying pan on to one of the oven's hot plates, spooned in a dollop of soft lard and a generous slab of beef. 'I'll show you.'

They went through a doorway into a long gloomy room that had been converted from a rear veranda. There were no windows except for one at the far end, which was fixed and hardly big enough for Dawson Cayne to squeeze through. There was also a door, but Jack saw it was locked and very substantial. He followed the Mexican to what was obviously an annexed bedroom. There was a single window, a pair of glass-panelled, heavily draped doors that led through to Kettle's study. The way Jack saw it, there was only one window to watch in the rear of the house.

Back in the kitchen, Ramon forked over the sizzling meat in the pan, half-smiled and added a generous helping of chili.

Not long afterwards, meat, eggs and biscuits were being consumed in the study.

'It's been a long while since someone handed me a platter of victuals,' Bream said favourably. 'I kind o' like it.'

Between mouthfuls, Jack had been outlining his simple plan;

' . . . then we fill every lantern we can lay hands on and hang them along the front and back verandas.'

'Like a jamboree. He'll blow 'em to pieces,' Bream said.

'So perhaps we'll know where he is,' Jack replied. 'Ramon, I need a good man in the kitchen. You're familiar with the sounds. Anything you don't like, just discharge that old smoke pole. Hec, you and Mr Kettle are responsible for these windows.'

'What about me?' Rico said, hauling himself on to one elbow.

'Same as Ramon. If you see someone you don't know — shoot 'em. The front's my area. So, let's set up those lanterns.'

The wick of the storm lamp spluttered in the curtain of rain that blew against the house. Jack cupped his hands and struck a fresh match. This time the flame caught and he lowered the glass chimney, turned up the flame and hung the lantern on one of the long tacks that Hector Bream had hammered in. Four more lanterns glowed above the damp boards of the front veranda.

Jack looked into the darkness of the home yard. He knew that if Cayne was already out there he might not make it back to the open doorway. With each step he took he tensed for the big bullet. In the doorway, with his back exposed to light from the flickering lanterns, he was the perfect target, if only for the shortest moment.

No, he told himself. He doesn't want to finish me like this . . . long range. He wants to be close . . . probably got something to say. Then he made it inside, kicking the door shut, cursing with relief.

The interior of the house was in darkness. The only light in the study belonged to the red tip of Ramon's cigarillo.

'I'm not stopping smoking for anyone,' he'd said. '*Nadie*. If anyone gets hit, it'll be me.'

'Talking of getting hit, if your man out there pokes out as much as his nose, he'll end up like a goddamn riddle,' Kettle said.

'That's good stuff. Remember, no matter what happens, to stay where you are. That way we won't kill each other.' Jack closed the door on them, walked steadily along the hall to the kitchen.

'Everything all right, Hec? Anything strange happened?'

'Yes . . . that is, no,' Bream replied from the darkness. Jack looked at the stove.

'Keep the gate shut. It'll be a fair old glow in this dark,' he advised and went back to the front of the house.

He pulled up an armless chair and sat facing the windows, his battered rifle resting across his knees. He could see the falling rain glinting through the swaying beams of yellow light outside. A big moth struck the hot chimney glass of the nearest lantern, immediately fell from sight.

It's the light. What I hoped would draw Cayne, Jack mused.

He had taken Connie's lucky charm from his pocket, was squeezing it tight in the palm of his left hand when he heard the shattering of glass. A lantern exploded and the echo of a rifle shot rolled across the dark yard.

He rushed to a window, half-expecting to see the flash of gunfire. But the study door opened and Kettle and Ramon strode in.

'That was one of the lanterns,' Kettle said, worriedly and unnecessarily.

'Did you see where the shot came from?' Ramon asked.

'No, and he can pick them off, one by one. Like a goddamn shooting gallery. Hec was right.' Irate, Jack turned, looked around. 'He's trying to faze us. We've all got to stay calm. Just stay where you are and keep still and you can shoot at anything that doesn't.'

Another shot sounded and through the open study doorway they saw a second lantern black out.

'Go on then,' Jack snapped.

The next shot came from behind the house. Again glass shattered, but this time a bullet struck an inner wall. Jack cursed.

'Hec,' he called loudly. 'Stay low and get out of the way of those windows. Make the son of a bitch come closer. He's firing hopefully.'

The quiet then held for a few minutes.

'Why don't he shoot?' Kettle called from the study. 'I can't stand this not knowing when or from where.'

'Yeah, he knows that. Don't do what he knows you're going to do.'

'So let's go out there. Why wait for him?'

'Because that's exactly what he wants. Us, on his shooting ground. Stay put. Hang on to your nerve.'

There was a longer silence, then Ralph Kettle called out from the study:

'Do you reckon he's pulled out?'

'No.'

'Could he have run out of bullets?'

'Not run out, no.'

'I'm coming through,' the rancher announced and his shadowy figure appeared in the low lamplight.

'Keep away from the windows,' Jack muttered. Kettle stopped moving.

'If he's still there, why doesn't he start shooting? He knows where we are.' He asked.

'So far he's made his shots count. With .50-calibre slugs he hasn't got a whole arsenal with him. Calm down for Chris'sakes. It looks like he's getting to you.'

Kettle lapsed into silence, then with a heavy sigh he turned and went back to his study.

Jack could hear Rico mumbling to

himself. It sounded like he was echoing Kettle's sentiments. He laughed sombrely. The night was Cayne's chosen time. Come to think of it, darkness had been his life as a child . . . standing behind others . . . in their shadow, saying little.

'Jack, it's me,' Hector Bream said.

'What is it, Hec?'

'You got matches left?'

Jack moved out of the line of the windows, turned his back and snapped a match alight. Bream leaned forward, grunted as his small cigar caught light.

'If Ramon can I can — even if I don't,' he said with a thin smile.

'You can smoke it back in the kitchen,' Jack said.

'I don't think so, Jack. I've had enough of this waiting.'

'Is this some sort of conspiracy, Hec? What are you saying?'

'I'd rather go out there.'

'Yeah, of course you would. On your own against Cayne?'

'It's better than waitin' for him to

come an' get me . . . us.'

'It's a heroic thought, is what it is, Hec. Dumb, but heroic. How's you dying going to make it easier for the rest of us? We're all safer and best off by you being where you're needed. Not face down in the mud.'

'I could slip out the back way.'

'It won't help, goddamnit,' Jack almost snapped back.

'OK, I tried. Thanks for the light.' Bream stepped away into the darkness of the hallway, returned frustrated to his kitchen.

Jack found himself holding his breath as he listened for any sound Bream might be making. But he couldn't afford to get jumpy. He'd half-expected Cayne to have found a way into the kitchen while Bream had been away.

'No one's going out there tonight,' he asserted as Kettle reappeared in the doorway.

'I've been thinking,' the rancher said. 'Depending on what he loads that gun with, if he got close enough he could probably take out the corner posts of the house. Where'll we be then, with half the roof falling in on us?'

'Hell!' Jack exclaimed, raising his eyes to the ceiling. He suddenly recalled Cayne's escape from the hayloft of the burning livery. Tonight he could enter Kettle's ranch house by coming in that way. With the sound of the drumming rain drowning out most other noise, it wasn't impossible. So far the man had been coming and going wherever and whenever he pleased.

20

The wind had picked up. It had pushed the rain, made a hissing sound against the walls of the house.

Rising from the chair, Jack felt cold, thought the study fire must have died down or gone out. He walked to the doorway, saw the figure of Ramon stretched out on the carpet.

'He's asleep,' Kettle said from the desk. 'Lucky old him.'

Yeah, not like us, Jack thought.

'What's up?' Rico called from the cot.

'Nothing. How'd you feel?' Jack said quietly.

'Weak as my boss's whiskey. How much longer you playing blind man's buff?'

'It's not a game, Rico. And we're in no position to make the first move.'

'Listen, gringo man, I was nearly

dead yesterday and still my nerves are better than yours. He's laughing at you, just as I am. Two gunshots and you've all turned to shaky men.'

'Quiet, Rico,' Kettle said. 'Being nearly dead's allowing your mouth to say tough things. What Jack says is right.'

Sitting by the fireplace, Ramon stirred. He got to his feet, looked down at the dying fire.

'Why did you let me sleep, señor?' he said.

'Why not? Nothing's happened.' Kettle replied.

'And nothing will,' Rico muttered irritably.

Jack frowned and glanced at the window.

'Oh no?' he said, moving forward quickly. 'Then what the hell's this?'

Beyond the beams of the hanging lanterns he could see that the bunkhouse was on fire, the flames driven low and flat by the vigorous wind. Immediately Ramon, Kettle and Hector Bream stepped in closer to the window. The yard was more visible under the spread of flame and Bream pointed.

'Look. Over by the corral. It's him,' he rasped.

A horseman had emerged from the deep shadow, was riding slow and sure towards the house. Bream and Ramon raised their guns.

'*Quien?* What's going on?' Rico yelled through the doorway.

'Shut up,' Jack shouted, reaching out to grab Bream's rifle. 'Don't shoot,' he added, staring intently at the figure on the horse. 'That's Walt Bishop. The horse has brought him back.'

The horse halted in the middle of the yard, as though Bishop had hauled rein.

How the hell did he do that? Jack thought, peering hard at what he could see of the man in the saddle. The clothes looked like Bishop's, but the horse remained still, apparently under some sort of control. Looking along the barrel of his old musket, Ramon took aim.

'If he's dead, this won't hurt,' he breathed as he pulled the trigger.

The heavy body jerked under the impact of the bullet, but didn't fall. Giving a toss of its head, the horse reared up, stomped at the yard mud with its foreleg.

'It should've bolted,' Kettle hissed. 'It's being held in check.'

'Not by Bishop it's not,' Ramon said. He reached for Bream's rifle, issued a vivid Spanish curse as the horse broke into a trot toward them. Sighting fast, he squeezed off a shot, then another. But the body just shuddered in the saddle. They could all now see the face clearly in the light from the veranda lanterns.

'It's Walt all right,' Kettle said.

'*Oye*. Someone tell me what the hell's going on,' Rico yelled from the study.

'Keep quiet, else we'll send you to find out,' Kettle shouted back. Jack's gaze was concentrated on the approaching horseman.

'He's there,' he said slowly and in awe. 'He's sitting behind Bishop.'

At that moment the horse leapt into a gallop as it neared the window.

Jack swung up his Winchester, but Cayne was already firing. The big bullet ripped through the open window, pulsed the air within inches of Jack's forehead, making him swing around, cursing against the darkness as he fell.

'Damn you to hell, Cayne!'

★ ★ ★

'You OK, Jack?'

Jack's vision cleared and he saw Kettle's weathered face hovering above him. There was a dull throbbing pain in his head and the rancher's face blurred again. He blinked some focus back, and in the match flame he saw the faces of Hector Bream and Ramon.

'We thought he'd got you,' Bream said.

'He nearly did. How long have I been out?' Jack asked.

'Not long. About fifteen minutes.'

'Did you see him?'

'For a moment after he fired.'

Jack attempted to get up from the carpet. 'What the hell's got into me?' he said.

Kettle leaned in closer. 'At a guess son, I'd say a crazy jumble of nerves, confusion and fatigue.'

'Better than death, I suppose. Do you know where he is now?'

'After he'd galloped by he just vanished. Hasn't been a sight or sound of him since.'

'Goddamnit! You shouldn't be here watching over me,' Jack shouted, pushing up to his feet. 'He could have got in anywhere. He could be here right now. Hec, lock that door.'

Bream gave a hollow laugh. 'He couldn't be anywhere in here. I'll go check out the rooms.' The cook moved away quickly and they heard him moving, looking, around.

'No one here. I'm goin' to the kitchen,' he called out.

The man's footsteps got quieter, then they heard the latch go on the kitchen door. Bream called out again, but they couldn't make out what he said. Then there was another sound, as if the door was slamming shut.

'What the hell's that?' Kettle gasped.

'I don't know,' Jack grated.

The men froze at the sound of footsteps on the veranda. They levelled their guns, turning towards the light from the flickering lanterns.

A figure stood silhouetted against the window and Jack lowered his rifle.

'It's Hec,' he said. Then he shouted, 'Are you crazy? I almost blew your head off.'

Bream gave his nervous laugh, then pushed up the window to climb inside. He had just lifted his left leg across the sill when his body gave a mighty judder and arched backwards to the veranda. His foot twitched once, then went still.

The shot was deafening in the darkness, ringing in their ears. The men inside the house threw themselves away from the window, gasping with shock.

'Get down,' Jack yelled. 'He's somewhere to the left.'

They hit the floor a second before the window shattered and bullet after bullet hammered into the interior walls.

Then there was silence, complete utter silence.

'Now we know he's not anywhere inside. That was to keep us down,' Jack said. 'But it probably means he's on the move.' He stood beside the shattered window and its frame, looked out on the motionless features of Hector Bream. 'He's dead,' he muttered. 'He went out through the kitchen door. I can see it's still open.'

'I'll go shut it,' Ramon said.

Jack peered around the yard, considered the four dead and one wounded. Had the quest for a vengeance been taken over by the sheer visceral satisfaction of killing?

'Well not by me it hasn't,' he said to no one in particular.

Rico ripped out some cuss words.

'He's going to kill you all. It's like the goddamn Alamo, with me left as old Jim Bowie.'

Kettle was trying not to listen. 'Ramon's taking his time,' he said. 'How long's it take to check a goddamn door? You don't think — ?' Jack grabbed the rancher's shoulder.

'I'll go take a look. We know he can't be far.'

'It's OK. I think I heard him.'

The men stood frozen, listening for a sound above the heavy soughing of the wind. Jack called the Mexican's name.

'*Sí*. I'm coming,' came the reply. The door opened and Ramon entered the study. 'Now it's locked,' he said.

'What time is it?' Rico asked.

'About one,' Jack answered dully.

'First light's sometime after five,' Kettle said.

'Do we leave Hec like that?' Ramon wanted to know.

'He's not bothered,' Rico said.

'*No me gusta*,' the old Mexican insisted. 'We can't leave him like a dog.'

245

'We're not, but there's no choice,' Jack muttered wearily. 'We'll bury him tomorrow.'

At half past three Jack shivered, shook himself more alert. He'd meant to stay sharp but events were catching up with him. The others were silent too, with fatigue or on edge with fear, and he couldn't blame them. They probably thought they were going to die anyway. It made no difference if it happened in their sleep. For a couple of hours Jack had been pondering on little more than Cayne: the man's reasons for such prolonged and shocking killing.

Was it all about a vindictive wish from a man on his deathbed? A tragedy to right an imaginary wrong? Had living really become that deranged?

These thoughts all started to put Jack's own motives into question, to set his search for Annie's killer into perspective. He was so deep in his mix of thoughts that he missed the beginning of the sound. He only became aware of it during a brief lull in the wind. It was a drawn-out, grating sound, the creak of wood slowly splintering apart, and it came from the rear of the house. Jack touched Kettle and Ramon on their shoulders.

'I think he's come back, and he's trying to get in,' he said when they stirred.

'Yes. It sounds like in the kitchen,' Ramon whispered after they'd listened for a moment. 'He might be torching the inside.'

'I've thought of that,' Jack said. 'We'd put it out . . . probably him along with it. Besides, he'd have to find oil. If he's tossed a torch in, we'd have heard. No, he's back there waiting. I'll give him something worth waiting for.'

'Like what? What do you mean?' Kettle asked.

'Me. It's about time I went for him. You two stay here, no matter what. *Comprende?*'

'Yes, we understand, Jack. Remember, when you come back identify yourself. You've returned me my big fifty, remember.'

'Yeah,' Jack replied, smiling thinly. 'And I'll leave my trusty Winchester here as well. I want to be close enough to see his eyes.' With that, he shut the door behind him, moved cautiously into the hallway.

He stopped at the door that led to the kitchen and flexed his shoulders and the fingers of his right hand. He prodded the door with the barrel of his Colt and stepped quietly forward; he stared blankly at the outer, open doorway.

It was the door that Bream was supposed to have closed. Jack was trying to figure out what had happened when there came the sound of a smashing of glass and the deafening boom of Kettle's big rifle.

Jack backed away as another shot punched the air, then another and another. His hand wrenched the door open and he staggered back into the short hallway. The double doors of the study were wide open and Ramon's body was stretched across the desk.

'I got him . . . put a bullet in him,' Kettle gasped from his position on the floor. 'Mind you, he got me too, but I'll live. You just make sure he don't.'

Jack struck a match and lit the lamp above the stone mantelpiece. He looked around the room, saw that Rico's face was set with a grimace. Blood oozed slowly from the whole of the upper part of his body, but his right hand was still clutched around the handle of a thin-bladed skinning knife.

'He really did think he was at the Alamo,' Jack mumbled.

'Go get Cayne, son,' the rancher repeated. 'This ranch has had enough.'

Jack saw his quarry. The man was way ahead, cutting a trail that led from the oak-wooded grassland up into the Sierras.

Up until then Jack had been chasing the sounds of a lone horse. But now he had something visible to track at that distance, even making out the corn-coloured hair that brushed the killer's shoulders. He spurred his mount on through the conifers, rode higher to a world of rock plants and grey stone. He paused to stare at the mountains that towered high above him, a narrow track that wound upwards, in and out of hard ridges.

There was a trace of blood here and there, and he recalled Kettle saying he'd put a bullet in him. Jack assumed any hit from a Sharps big-fifty would be devastating.

He cleared a ridge, reined in to glance at his backtrail. You're not getting behind me, you son of a bitch, he thought. From there on he'd climb on foot. OK, because he was chasing a man half-roasted and carrying an ounce of lead inside him. 'How difficult can that be,' he muttered icily.

He ground-hitched his horse and started up a stony slope. He lost his footing on the small loose boulders, slipping a few feet until he dug his heels in. Lying on his side, squinting against the light, he saw Cayne's riderless horse off to the right of the grade.

The sun rose in the sky, but suddenly the wind died and the silence was eerie. Sweat was running down the side of his face, trickling between his shoulder blades. The glitter from the crystalline rock around him almost stung his eyes as he worked his way up and across the slope. At last he reached the ledge and saw fresher, dark bloodstains. Then he saw that the ledge led only to another, steeper slope. He cursed, took a breath and moved slowly, carefully, up towards the lip.

Dawson Cayne was standing between two wedges of upward-slanting rock. Outlined against the sky, and no more than thirty feet away, he was unmoving but taller and more terrifying a figure than Jack had witnessed at any time before.

Jack got to his feet and stood motionless. He calmed his breathing, controlled the tremble of his right hand. So, am I going to remain steady? he thought.

'The hell I am,' he said, levelling his Colt and firing.

He saw every detail of the man's face, as harsh and as hard as the rock itself. The burned hands and fingers seemed like talons as they clutched the big bore rifle.

'I haven't got the words, Cayne,' he called out, firing again. 'There's a big bird been following me around. He can have you.' He actioned his Colt and fired a third and final time.

Jack sat down and drew out the old picture from the Tucson Messenger; the group of children waving flags at a summer street party. He tore it twice, then tossed the pieces up into the cold, twisting wind.

★　★　★

One week later, Jack sat at a corner table in a Whitewater tavern. He was drinking cheap barleycorn and coffee, thinking about his future.

He pulled out and checked his

252

stemwinder, looked towards the front door. In fifteen minutes he was scheduled to catch a stage out to the border. After that, it was on to Bowie and a 100-mile ride west to Tucson. Returning to the farm was a gloomy prospect, but hopefully it would bring some sort of finale to his chase. He glanced at his watch again, got to his feet and moved towards the door. Ralph Kettle and his daughter were walking towards him from the direction of the sanatorium.

'Shouldn't be long now,' he said, as they approached.

'I'm sorry,' Kettle said. 'We've a few more people than you to say goodbye to. No offence.'

Jack looked quizzical. 'None taken. But goodbye? I don't understand.'

'We're going home,' Connie answered.

'Flagstaff?'

Kettle grinned, tugged at his arm sling.

'It's where we came from. Always was the best grazing in the state.'

'When?' Jack asked, looking for something in Connie's face.

'Couple of weeks or so. Soon as I get shot of the RK. You'll be welcome any time, Jack. As long as you don't bring any one with you. No more offence, of course.'

Jack nodded in acceptance. Briefly, he thought of saying his enemies were all dead.

'No more taken,' he offered.

'Hmm.' The man's rheumy blue eyes were fixed on Jack. 'Well, you've got your mare back, and we're keeping a fine pair of breed buckskins to take with us,' he said. 'Likely be the start of a fine new herd. What more could anyone want, eh?'

'Family and friend's are always a good idea,' Jack suggested. He glanced down the street, saw the stage rolling slowly around the corner and decided it was a suitable time to move.

'The ranch will be called TK. That's Two Kettles, and the nearest town's Lemmon,' Connie called out.

Heading for the depot, Jack turned and waved. He had his saddle-bags in his left hand and Connie's lucky charm in his right.

'I'll remember,' he shouted back.

MASSACRE AT RED ROCK

Jack Martin

Liberty Jones is tired of war. Now he just wants to be left in peace, but trouble has a way of finding him. Riding into the town of Red Rock to escape a marauding tribe of Indians, any hopes of safety he had are soon dispelled. The town is under military command, facing a gathering of tribes who are determined to drive people from the town and reclaim their land. Liberty and his band of townspeople must face impossible odds before blood runs deep in the streets of Red Rock . . .

THE WIZARD OF WAR SMOKE

Michael D. George

Marshal Matt Fallen and his deputy Elmer Hook have never seen War Smoke so busy. People are gathering for the opening night of the Tivoli theatre, and top of the bill is the famed Mezmo, an illusionist who can reputedly mesmerize anyone into doing his bidding. When a series of murders occurs before the show begins, Fallen is convinced that Mezmo is to blame. But as more men fall victim to the mysterious assassin, can Marshal Fallen outwit the Wizard of War Smoke and discover the truth behind the slayings?